Gambler's Fallacy

Judith Cowan

Gambler's Fallacy

The Porcupine's Quill

CANADIAN CATALOGUING IN PUBLICATION DATA

Cowan, Judith Elaine
Gambler's fallacy

ISBN 0-88984-225-6

I. Title.

PS8555.O8575.G34 2001   C813'.541   C2001-901536-4
PR9199.3.C667G34 2001

Published by The Porcupine's Quill,
68 Main Street, Erin, Ontario NOB ITO.
Readied for press by John Metcalf; copy-edited by Doris Cowan.
Typeset in Bauer Bodoni, printed on Zephyr Antique laid,
and bound at The Porcupine's Quill Inc.

Represented in Canada by the Literary Press Group.
Trade orders are available from General Distribution Services.

We acknowledge the support of the Ontario Arts Council,
and the Canada Council for the Arts for our publishing program.
The financial support of the Government of Canada
through the Book Publishing Industry Development Program
is also gratefully acknowledged.

I   2   3   4   •   03   02   01

Canada

Acknowledgements

Several of the stories in this collection have been previously published, either as they appear here or in a somewhat revised version.

'The Best Time of the Night' first appeared as 'Dans la rue Sainte-Angèle' in *Matrix* Number 39, Spring 1992.

'Laiah and the Sun King' appeared in *The Canadian Forum*, Volume 78, Number 884, December 1999.

'The Unknown Poet' was published in *The Malahat Review*, Number 119, June 1997.

Table of Contents

Et vous que je découvre enfin
Au bout de l'horrible chemin,
Vous que je ne pouvais prévoir
Mais qu'au fond de ma destinée,
D'une tendresse résignée,
Je dus chérir sans le savoir...

Clément Marchand
'Paroles aux compagnons'
Les soirs rouges, 1947

The Launching

At the top of the steps, the heavy door thunked back in the wet wind. It caught and shuddered on its jointed restraining rod. When Raymonde looked up, she saw large human shapes outlined against the pink light of the March evening. The last one in the group was tugging the door shut behind them. There are only three steps down from the rue Bonaventure into the Café Zénob and two people had clomped down them and were already upon her, bringing a damp gust with them. The dampness itself was special because it meant that the cold had broken. The temperature had risen above freezing and the early, ugly, exciting spring was on its way. Raymonde felt a tightness in her chest, and a quiver that might have been happiness or might have been stress. Russell was having the first book launch of the season, and here they were, not the first arrivals, but the most imposing.

Smiling through the smoke from the bar, trying hard not to be seen shivering in the blast from the street, Raymonde recognized Russell's mother at the centre of the new arrivals. Madame Paradis was a big woman and she flourished down the steps in an unzipped parka and a many-layered peasant skirt of unidentifiable ethnicity. Before Raymonde could take the initiative and kiss her, she had seized her son's mistress by her small sharp shoulders and planted firmly proprietorial kisses on both her cheeks. There was a hint of admonition in her grasp, as if to say, Take that, *ma fille*, and try to behave yourself! What she actually said was:

'Bonsoir, Raymonde, comme c'est beau, quelle belle occa-

9

sion! Et la neige est presque partie, on est sortis sans bottes pour la première fois!'

The snow was gone, at least from the sidewalks. Madame Paradis, newly bootless and lightfooted with spring, did not bother to introduce the two hulking men with her, much younger than she was, and perfect strangers to Raymonde. She was already past and on her way towards the rear. Raymonde would certainly have kissed both of the big men regardless, anything to make Russell's launch a success, but they sidestepped around her and got across to the bar unkissed.

Outside, the deep granular snowbank which had covered the terrasse of the Zénob since January was sublimating into the tumultuous air. The Ides of March had come and the hideous life-denying winter was over, forgotten as if there would never be another. The day's cold boisterous rain had blown itself out by five o'clock and now, from under the clouds, the setting sun was casting a weird lateral illumination across the street. Its theatrical rays glamourized the statue of Maurice Duplessis on his pedestal beside the Manoir de Niverville and gleamed back from the small blank windowpanes of the old manor house. More people could be heard out there, excited by the pink light and calling to each other against the wind. Then they were banging in through the door and crowding down into the bar.

Raymonde was relieved and exhilarated to see so many of them because it meant a good beginning for Russell's book, the windy start of a new season, full of hope. Looking up the steps at the darkening rectangle of sunset, she knew that his publisher had chosen the perfect date for the launching.

So she stood in the chilly draft in her silk dress and patent leather shoes, smiling, chatting, eagerly kissing people. Between greetings, she scanned the room. The Zénob is small and low-ceilinged. As always, it was full of cigarette smoke and Raymonde, who had never smoked in her life, was slightly euphoric already with second-hand nicotine. She didn't really mind. It helped her to feel less out of place.

At the far end of the bar the regulars had congregated, all smoking, and only occasionally looking up to acknowledge an acquaintance among the crowd who'd come for the launching. Several of the founding Bohemians had actually grown grey in that spot, posted in the corner by the sound system and the kitchen door. In its beginnings, the Zénob had been the actors' bar, and the old gang were or had been the theatre crowd, actors and musicians, now mostly settled into government jobs, or teaching, or just drinking. There were one or two who had, except when actually hospitalized, spent every single Friday night in the Zénob for the past fifteen years. And they all knew Russell. Everyone knew Russell. But they didn't often speak to Raymonde. She was simply Russell's current woman. They'd seen others come and go.

A few of the younger crowd came down the steps and strode to the bar in their turn – tall, narrow-skulled twenty-some-things dressed in black, although not so many of them as on a Saturday night. They certainly had nothing to say to Raymonde, and moved across through the layers of smoke as if on a different plane of existence. It was enough for them to know that this sort of thing was for the old crowd, the last shrivelled remnants of Trois-Rivières's previous counter-culture, dating from the eighties or even the seventies. One of them did meet Raymonde's glance, but only for an instant. He gave her a cool smile before turning back to his friends at the bar. They tolerated and expected to be tolerated.

And Russell was excellent with them. He knew how to play up to their expectations and their misapprehensions. For them, he presented a well-crafted caricature of himself, never told them that they hadn't understood and never tried to explain what the nineteen-seventies were really like.

But where was Raymonde in all this? She was with Russell,

and that was the sole reason for her ever having set foot in this
bar, where at the moment she was hanging on out of sheer loyalty. Where was he anyway? Looking around, she spotted him
at the back of the room. His bald head stuck up out of the
crowd, its shifting reflections transmitting the energy of whatever it was he was lecturing them about. She wished that he'd
talk to her with that kind of passion but knew better than to
expect it. Raymonde was much too grown up to be one of the
young crowd while still a few years too young to belong to the
old theatre crowd.

She hung her head and noticed her shoes, suddenly saw them
as all wrong, their formal bows of corded ribbon flecked with
sparkles of gold lamé. Party shoes. How foolish. No one else here
was wearing party shoes. Why hadn't she seen this earlier?
Around her shoes were other feet in heavy black shoes, shoes
with platform soles, even army boots. Well, she did have boots.
Raymonde's fleece-lined, zip-up snowboots, together with her
velvet shoe bag, were right here on the floor somewhere, under
the table with the coats. But she knew that her snowboots, salt-
stained and gummy-soled, wouldn't be right either. At the start
of the seventies Raymonde had been a serious-minded teenager,
planning to study dental hygiene and hoping later on to marry
and have children and stay at home. But marry whom? Marry
what? Her adolescent anticipations had taken a lot for granted.
Somehow none of that had come to pass. Dental hygiene had
turned out to be too technical for her and the marriage market
too competitive. The teenaged Raymonde (and then twentyish,
and then thirtyish) had gone on expecting the husband candi-
date until her fortieth birthday, several years ago. Along the way
she'd one or two bad disappointments, which she had decided
not to think about any more.

Instead she held her head up, took her vitamins, dyed her
hair, and looked resolutely forward. She worked off and on for
the Ministère de la Culture, at contract jobs. At the university,

she taught French conversation to the English-speakers who regularly descend upon Trois-Rivières for French immersion. She expended her maternal solicitude on the poet Russell Paradis and, by extension, on his books. His literary creations were his progeny and therefore hers as well. She was there for him and for the whole Paradis clan. Maybe that was the reason for her slight feeling of breathlessness. It was stage fright.

'We couldn't find anywhere to park by the post office so that meant we had to come all the way back up and park under city hall,' yelled someone over her head.

She was reasonably sure that that was one of Russell's brothers-in-law, with a niece and nephew in tow. They pulled off their coats and threw them onto the heap behind her, just pausing to say *'Salut, Raymonde,'* before pushing into the crowd. She couldn't remember their names but obviously they knew her.

Madame Paradis was by this time queening it in a corner, two tables from the microphone where Russell would read. One of the pair of bulky, impassive men who'd come in with her had fetched her a glass of what looked like rum and Coke and had then rejoined his partner at the bar. They were probably family but it was never easy to tell. Madame Paradis was supposed to have a husband somewhere, and certainly Russell made occasional allusions to a father, but Raymonde had never seen him and neither had anyone else she knew. His mother, on the other hand, was seen everywhere, and with a startling variety of men. She claimed to be an artist.

'Know what she used to paint?'

Raymonde jumped. Denis, the publisher's man, had come through the door while she was staring back through the crowd. He had a cardboard box of books in his hands.

'They told me she painted portraits.'

Denis threw her a glance as he set the box down on the floor. He crouched over it.

'Ever seen them? She painted all right, on black velvet ...'
Talking into the box, Denis pulled its flaps open, '... and
always of Indian maidens with long black braids, doe-eyed in
doeskin ...' then sat back and looked up at Raymonde, his
bony wrists hanging for a moment between his long knees, '...
and lots of white doeskin fringes.'

He bit off the word 'fringes' as if it were an obscenity and
Raymonde laughed, but cautiously.

'She used to call them her *sauvagesses* ...' he went on.

'Oh, no ...'

That couldn't be correct. Raymonde waited.

'... and when the university came along and opened a *Mod-
ule des arts plastiques*, she even taught a course or two, in what
she was calling *l'art aborigène*, until one day an Abenaki stu-
dent showed up in class ...'

Denis pulled a metal cash box out of the carton of books and
straightened up with it. He dragged a small table over and set
the cash box on it. Raymonde tried not to stare across at
Madame while they talked about her.

'He was offended?'

Denis snorted.

'He laughed and laughed, but then he went to the university
administration and got someone to take a look at her stuff for
the first time. So her teaching career sort of quietly tapered off
after that.'

Raymonde ventured a longer look at Madame.

'Well, I ... I really thought she was a painter ...'

When amused, Denis indulged in a tight rictus that might
have been a smile but looked more like pain or disgust than
merriment.

'That's what she thinks too ...'

And he turned his back before Raymonde could continue,
leaving her with the books while he went across to say hello to
the lady, by whom he was graciously received.

Watching him go, Raymonde hoped she hadn't said any-thing wrong, or laughed when she shouldn't have. Denis was always straightforward and apparently objective, but sardonic about it. Poets and all other artists were the raw materials of someone's marketing enterprise, for better or for worse. According to Russell, Denis had originally come from an MBA programme at the university. He'd dropped out when he was hired to do public relations, years ago, for a summer theatre festival, then had found his niche in the promotion and mar-keting of books. This he did with the selfless single-mindedness that a man of an earlier generation might have given to a reli-gious vocation. To Raymonde, Denis looked as if he were always wearing the same suit on his lanky frame, although it was clean and presentable, the front of it invariably filled with a white shirt and a plain tie. *Business*, that was what his body language, his expression, his whole attitude declared: this is a business and I am a businessman. Like any other.

And apparently he was. At any rate he was known to be wonderfully good at selling books. Then loud voices from the bar called Raymonde's attention away from the confabulation still in progress between Denis and Madame Paradis.

'Gone down and taken a look at the river today?'

'The ice is breaking up ...'

'Yes, no, but I mean tonight, just in the last hour ...'

'It's going out fast...?!'

'Going out fast and coming up faster. The water'll be up over the port by midnight!'

The man predicting the flood was one of Madame Paradis's companions. Tight-lipped, he held up the beer glass in his hand, bent his head to one side and waggled both pessimisti-cally.

At the bar the prediction of an impending flood was greeted with enthusiasm. There was a ragged chorus of drunken cheers. Flooding was a happy disruption of the boring world's normal boring activities, a welcome sign of disorderly spring.

'It's spring, it's spring, *c'est le printemps enfin...!*' the drinkers shouted. Spring at last.

And they hoisted their glasses and bottles, bashing them together. Who cared if the paper companies' sheds were water-logged, if international shipping was prevented from tying up at the port, or if town traffic had to detour around the rue Notre-Dame to avoid sloshing through washouts of unknown depth? Flooding meant thaw and the thaw meant an end to cold and shivering, and a fresh upwelling of sex hormones. Hurray, hurray.

Through the din, the unavoidable music and the cries of recognition and welcome and flattery, Raymonde stiffened her spine and turned her attention back to the door. When Denis reappeared he was carrying a glass of red wine, which he held out to her with an enquiring look. She shook her head at it and asked him about the two men who'd come in with Madame Paradis.

'Who are those two guys over at the bar?'

Denis looked the pair over. One was bald, with a large moustache, the other had short hair and a smaller moustache.

'Not sure. Look like undercover cops, don't they? Or body-guards. Anybody important here?'

'They came in with Russell's mother.'

'Oh well then, not cops. They must be family. They're *her* bodyguards. Can't expect the queen bee to venture out all on her own.'

Raymonde felt the secret tightness in her chest dissolving into a frisson, maybe of envy. She did sentry duty in the draft at the door while Russell's mother was provided with a team of escorts. But she quickly suppressed her resentment because more people were on their way down the steps and it was her duty to speak to them. The launch was turning out to be a real success. Coats continued to pile up on the tall bar table beside the door and a heap of them had slid down onto a chair.

Denis gave himself the glass of wine that Raymonde hadn't wanted, then got down to business. He moved some of the coat-slide over and drew a chair up to the table with the cash box, just behind Raymonde's post. He opened the carton and began pulling out handfuls of Russell's book. Its title was *Ater-moiements*, a word that Raymonde understood to mean stallings or evasions or something. Although she didn't like it, she hadn't tried to argue with Russell about it. It was his title and he wanted it. He wouldn't have listened to her anyway. This was his fifth collection of poems and he enjoyed respect and a growing celebrity. He knew what he was doing. So did Denis. He laid out copies of *Atermoiements* in a fan-shaped spread in front of him, with the cash box at its base. Then he sat back. He took a thin black cigarette out of a small flat tin case. Impassively, lighting it, he stared across it at Raymonde and gave her a sample of that tight grin. They were both on duty. He was there to sell the book, she was there to greet the public as they trooped in, except that the event was hardly public. No one was really a stranger. Even people Raymonde didn't recognize probably knew her and would expect her to know them. Trois-Rivières is like that. So she kissed them and expressed enthusiasm at seeing them even if she couldn't remember who they were. If they veered off without submitting to being kissed, she tried not to worry about it. Naturally there were always undercurrents. She'd been with Russell for only three years. There were family stories and of course tales from other sources, general gossip hinting at past girlfriends and half-buried antagonisms that she could know nothing about.

But if kissing Raymonde was more or less *facultatif*, getting past Denis was difficult. Most of those entering had come in response to a printed invitation, which included a ticket good for one free glass of wine. A free buffet had also been laid on. Between the invited guests coming in out of the wind and the spread of food stood the table with Denis and the stack of *Atermoiements.* As they came in, naturally most people felt obligated at least to take a look at the book. They'd pick up a copy and open it at random, read a few lines. Then, holding it in their hands, inevitably some of them would hesitate, probably fearing that they'd be seen as rude if they put it down again and moved on. It would look as if they didn't like whatever it was that they'd just read, so a good number of them handed over the money and bought the book. Immediately after that they stuck it into a pocket or a bag without taking another glance at it.

Raymonde was careful to avert her eyes from these brief scenarios in order not to appear pushy.

Two English-looking girls, not ones that Raymonde knew but obviously language exchange students from the campus, came down the steps and halted, wide-eyed. Perhaps they thought it was a private party. They weren't far wrong but Raymonde grabbed them before they could turn and flee. She recognized their situation and kissed them both, if not quite as possessively as Madame Paradis had kissed her.

'Mais, OUI!' she said, speaking extra clearly, *'entrez, ENTREZ...! Il faut que les gens VIENNENT ...'* while more arrivals pushing in behind the girls propelled them towards the bar.

Relaxing, the two girls smiled dizzily and went with the crowd. Holy shit, this was real French immersion. Raymonde turned back to the door and went on with her work.

'Salut, Denis, bonsoir André (smack, smack), *ça va bien Nicole? C'est beau, c'est bien, continue comme ça. Tiens, bonsoir Stéphane ...'*

The two girls, in their innocence, had walked right past the book table but the people following were caught. Denis sold two books, gave them their change, tilted his chair back, picked up his little black cigarillo or whatever it was and inhaled importantly. Raymonde also took a deep breath of aromatic second-hand smoke. She hoped that no one would ask her to discuss any of the poems and was happy to see that as soon as they'd paid for the book, the two couples pushed on into the room. Well, of course they wanted to get it signed by Russell. At the same moment she felt a colder blast of wind at her shoulder and glanced back up the steps.

The section of wet sky up there was completely dark now and Marc-André Malouin had just yanked the door open.

'*Bonsoir, Madame, bonsoir! Et comment va la maîtresse du grand homme?*' he shouted, swaggering down the stairs with the wind, leaving the door flapping open behind him.

Someone else closed it while Raymonde shrank back. *Maîtresse. Grand homme.* Part of that was true, or all of it, and part of it was simply embarrassing. Calling her *Madame*. Marc-André was a rival poet, a small man with a deep, sonorous voice. He cut through the babble while the great man's mistress did shiver, visibly. She smiled and hugged her arms around herself as Marc-André descended upon her. The kissing role was about to be reversed, she supposed, and for that she was alarmed and embarrassed. But Marc-André didn't try to kiss her on the face. Instead he seized her hand in his own square, hard-palmed one and kissed it lavishly. Raymonde gasped and stiffened. The warmth of his lips, and the furry feel of his moustache on the back of her hand had something animal about it, something that left her undecided whether she should laugh or scream.

Denis watched their exchange with his eyes narrowed, but that could have been because he was relighting his cheroot. Still, several people got past the table without looking at the books or being kissed. There was no more room for coats by the door and latecomers had to shove through to the rear of the bar, where there was a coat rack in the narrow passage along the back of the toilets. Ostentatiously, Marc-André pulled out a twenty-dollar bill and bought a book. With a wave of his hand, he turned away and joined the flow pushing towards the back.

Raymonde couldn't watch to see where he went because down the steps behind him had come a team from Radio-Canada, a tall woman with bright red hair and limp, expensive clothing, followed by a silent cameraman. They didn't need to be kissed but they did need to be introduced and oriented. Denis presented the woman with a book and was pointing out to her which one was Russell Paradis. He must have summoned them. Let him deal with them. This was her chance to go and get herself some white wine from the bar. Raymonde made her way through the crowd in that direction and was in time to see Pierre somebody-or-other, a *chansonnier* from the old crowd, abandon the little blonde he was talking to in the corner by the kitchen door and slide, literally slide down the bar towards the group who were discussing the rising water. That was where the English girls were. It turned out that Pierre had worked on the lake freighters. Immediately he was part of the conversation.

'There is a little bit of a tide in Trois-Rivières,' he informed them, 'last point on the St Lawrence where it can be detected. Maybe it's coming in now, so the water looks pretty high, but give it an hour or so and it'll be on the ebb. Then you'll see the water go down again.'

That much he said in French. Then, turning to the prettier of the two language students, he switched unexpectedly into English.

'Where're you from ...?'

The language shift caused the others at the bar to look away, including the man who had first mentioned the rising water, which of course was what Pierre wanted. The big pink-cheeked girl with the frizzy brown hair gave him an open-mouthed smile.

'Newfoundland,' she said, all eyelashes, 'we both are. My

name is Shawna and this here is my friend Megan.'

While Pierre was offering to buy Shawna a drink, one of the others said, in French, 'He doesn't know what he's talking about. The tide, if there is a tide, is out. Call Ports Canada. Ask them. They'll tell you.'

Pierre ignored them. He was asking Shawna about the tides around Newfoundland, and the icebergs in the harbour in St John's, and then about the pubs in that city.

Raymonde picked up her glass of wine and moved away. At the front of the bar but away from the entrance, under the windows, Alphonse Piché was sitting quietly, socratically, in the midst of a respectful empty space, talking or rather listening to three or four admirers. A small handsome man with a full head of white hair, Alphonse was Trois-Rivières's poet laureate, now eighty years old. He was known as a Scotch drinker and an admirer of women but he was also known to be slowing down. At the moment he had a glass of wine sitting untouched in front of him and was studying the pair of English girls at the bar. Raymonde went over to say hello to him.

'You like the looks of those *Anglaises?* You're going to make me jealous, Alphonse, running after all the young women.'

'Nowadays, *chère*, I just let them come to me,' he said, shifting his gaze to the woman from Radio-Canada, who was long-legged under her beige cashmere and suede.

The woman recognized him and wriggled past Raymonde to greet him, while her cameraman shouldered his camera and turned away towards the back of the room. He was sizing it up, the smoke, the noise level. They already had lots of film of Alphonse, from other occasions. Tonight it was Russell's turn to be recorded for posterity or for the archives at least. Maybe for the local evening news. Raymonde moved through the crowd, leaving the Radio-Canada woman warmly kissing Alphonse.

'Wow,' Megan was gushing to the man with the camera. She was braver about French than Shawna was. *'Quoi se passe?*

C'est quelqu'un célèbre ici à soir?' If he was filming a celebrity, she wanted to know who it was.

Raymonde shuddered but the man ignored Megan's rocky French. He was busy focusing his camera on the row of tall stools along the back wall, so Megan turned on her own stool and craned her neck after Marc-André, who was still talking his way through the crowd, heading in that direction. That was where Russell was receiving congratulations and signing books. He seemed to have stationed himself as far from the front door as possible, halfway between the toilets and the channel of coathooks leading to the back door. Already that door had been propped open to let out some of the smoke.

Russell Paradis was tall and strong-looking and still had long curly grey hair bursting out from behind his ears, but was completely bald on top. His lumpy cranium gleamed under a recessed ceiling light as he perched on a stool, smiling among his admirers. It was the young crowd who had surrounded him. They'd been told he was an intellectual, so they wanted to try out their ideas on him, and Russell was wise enough to listen, never mentioning his book. For their part, most of them were hoping to impress him with their own brilliance. Had they read any of his writing? Some of them might have, but for the rest, reading the man's work would have been superfluous when they could talk to him. They didn't expect to understand books and Russell seemed willing to leave it that way, to fulfil the stereotype of the writer as public figure.

Raymonde squeezed between the packed bodies and back to her post by the door. From across the room, she had glimpses of Russell blushing there, drinking Armagnac. There was something permanently youthful about him, especially when it came to things like the Armagnac. That was a recent affectation. For unknown reasons, he'd decided that it was more sophisticated than brandy, smoother somehow, and less likely to make him drunk. Tonight he'd had quite a lot of wine as well, so the effect was starting to show. Nevertheless he would read perfectly, no matter how drunk he was. At that, he was a pro, a veteran. And now Marc-André was over there, saying something to him.

She craned her neck to study the two men, Russell's big head sticking up out of the crowd, and an intermittent view of Marc-André's square shoulders planted in front of him, a foot shorter than he was. In spite of herself, Raymonde gave some thought to the way the girl from Newfoundland had pivoted on her stool to watch Marc-André pass. It certainly wasn't because of his size that she'd noticed him. It was his intensity. Dark-haired and dark-eyed, Marc-André Malouin moved at the centre of his own magnetic vortex, a force field that suggested nothing so much as a sort of permanent sexual indignation. He was always ruffled up. Maybe it was the combination of his small stature and his high energy level. He was intense. Now he was shouldering back through the crowd towards Raymonde.

'Funny thing,' he said, pushing into a space beside the coats, 'I've never noticed his phrenology before. First time I've really studied all the bumps. Is it the lighting? Wonder which one would be the bump of poetry.'

He stared across the room at Russell with unconvincing detachment. Denis, who had finished the red wine and was bringing himself back a beer, gave Marc-André a level look as he sat down again at the book table. Raymonde also understood exactly what Marc-André meant. She only wished that he hadn't said it. She set her glass down and walked away from him. She went to the bar and offered to help by passing a tray of sandwiches around. Marc-André followed her but it was only to get himself a beer.

Russell Paradis wasn't a bad poet. Not only did he have talent and imagination, but he belonged to a recognized stable, he was sure of getting publication grants, and he could be relied upon to produce his biennial book in time for the agreed-upon publication date without departing much from what was expected. His writing was what was sometimes called hermetic but that was good too. It was more difficult to criticize poems that created effect without really being understandable. And the effect of Russell's poetry was often admirable. Looked at objectively, *Atermoiements* was the honest production of an experienced artisan, an example of a recognized craft by a legitimate practitioner.

'Tell you what's wrong ...' said Denis to Raymonde, as she arrived back at the book table with the tray and offered him a sandwich.

'What's wrong ...?'

'Why Marc-André wants to talk about the bumps on Russell's head ...'

Denis took an egg sandwich from the tray.

'Oh! non vraiment ...'

Raymonde's knuckles whitened as she gripped the sandwich tray. Surely the subject could be dropped.

'No, wait, you don't read the literary mags. You don't always know what Russell's been publishing, do you? This past week there was a review by him of Marc-André's collection, you know, from last year ... and he said it was facile, said it lacked depth.'

Denis took a bite out of the sandwich. Raymonde exhaled a long breath.

'You know I stay out of all that.'

She also knew that Marc-André was published by a different house, or Denis would have kept his mouth shut.

He swallowed and said, 'Good idea. But anyway. I'm letting you know. Because you and I both know Marc-André. The way he acts. And of course you won't have read his book but it's just like him. Clear and up front and sort of aggressive. Anyone can understand it. So it's easy to pull it apart. All's fair in love and war and the publishing business. Especially poetry.'

'Russell isn't *anyone* ...'

'I didn't mean that. I'm just telling you that he didn't worry about sparing Marc-André's feelings.

'Russell's a good critic and a good writer,' she said, fiercely. Raymonde hadn't read Russell's book either but she wasn't going to admit that now. 'Everyone says so. He's not just a poet.'

'What does that mean? Not just a poet ... this is his launching, of a collection of poems, remember?'

Denis helped himself to two more sandwiches, quickly, before Raymonde could hoist the tray higher and carry it away to another table.

She wanted to be loyal to Russell, she was sincere in her belief in him and she knew that she was not alone. He was popular with the townspeople because he was one of them while at the same time fulfilling their notion of what an intellectual was supposed to be. If he was following in a tradition that had, when first launched by a small group of geniuses eighty or ninety years earlier, caused alarm and perplexity in the great centres of civilization, well, they hadn't heard about it. That was in foreign parts. *Les vieux pays.* What Russell was doing was an accepted form now, even in Trois-Rivières, and the foreign geniuses were long dead. Their revolt and their nonconformity had become a recognized standard to which Russell, elegantly, intelligently, was conforming. So tonight he could afford to be all openness and simplicity, all humble availability, while Marc-André was envious and made remarks about his bald head. Raymonde pressed on with the tray of sandwiches.

The mixture of people in the Zénob was proof of Russell's success. There were poets and there were civil servants who were *also* poets. There were actors, in and out of work. Several of the most successful of these survived by doing psychodramas for the cadets at the police college in Nicolet, convincingly portraying bank robbers, wife-batterers, confidence artists and assorted low-life psychopaths for embarrassed young men and women who had thought they wanted to be police officers. There was a blond woman with big hair and thin legs who sounded, from her voluble, English-accented French, to be an English Montrealer. She was explaining to one of the psychodramatists that she was a telephone systems specialist. She got a wry smile in return.

'Oh yes?' he said, 'so would that be what you mean by a call girl in English?'

'Oh, you *salaud*,' and the woman punched at him, 'you *know* what a call girl is. And you *know* that I'm a process engineer!'

'*Ah bon!* So that's what they're calling it now.'

And he winked past her at an intellectual plumbing parts wholesaler whom they both knew. The plumbing parts man gave them a preoccupied look and backed into the crowd.

There were musicians of all stripes. A classical oboist was there with a drummer from a percussion group calling themselves Les Gorilles aux Mains Rouges. A jazz cellist was describing to a Cégep administrator the course he was taking in how to become a travel agent. There were painters who were permanently on welfare and there was a weaver who worked part time with ex-convicts, teaching them to ride quarter horses. One of them had recently set fire to the barn, perhaps accidentally. There were some photographers and print-makers, not quite as penniless as the painters. There were lots of self-consciously pretty girls. There was a tight-lipped Swiss who worked for the Ministère de la Culture, handing out grants. He was treated with obsequious caution. There was a social historian who worked days in the paper mill. And there was an aspiring Olympian, a cross-country skier, who worked nights in the same paper mill. There was a jail guard. There were the Radio-Canada people and there was a small dark woman from Montréal, possibly from one of the newspapers, although no one was sure. There were various university types, whether students or professors it was hard to tell. There was a construction worker with a pony tail. He claimed that the tattoo on his biceps was a quotation from Rilke, but no one could actually read it, although several women had tried.

'Well, it's in German,' he said, 'the real German, they *told* me it was in the *real* German.'

And there were salesclerks and insurance agents and an American who had something to do with the Seaway and the grain elevators who had decided to be a patron of the arts as well. There were doctors' wives. There was even one doctor but he was also a poet.

'See that guy...?' the construction man was saying. 'That's *le sniffeux,* you know, the fetishist who smells women's feet!'

'No, where?!'

'Over there by the wall, I'm sure it's him.'

The dark-haired, clean-cut young man, if he was the foot fetishist, had been caught some years ago when he'd cornered an English professor at the university and imposed his nose upon her open-toed shoes. Tonight he was simply having a beer and talking quietly to another man.

'So just don't put your feet up anywhere near him ...'

'Don't worry ...'

With her feet planted firmly on the floor, in combat boots, this was the charming long-haired girl who had graduated in philosophy a few years back. Since then she had worked as a waitress in most of the downtown restaurants.

'*La philosophie...?*' she would say, when asked. 'Yes, it leads directly into waiting on tables.'

There were social workers and drug dealers and possibly a murderer or two. There was at least one dairy farmer. There was the man who owned a jeans store. There was a retired behavioural psychologist who restored British sports cars and there was a bookseller who played blues harmonica. And all this *beau monde* stood in a packed mass, talking, swilling wine and sizing each other up.

'That's Madame Paradis over there ...'

'*Madame* Paradis...?'

'His mother.'

'Oh. Where's his father?'

'Could be here somewhere. Wouldn't know. Think they're from the south shore. Lumber business.'

'Oh, the south shore,' said anyone who heard this.

Viewed from Trois-Rivières, the south shore was another world, peopled with welfare farmers and ceramics artists, retired policemen raising organic mutton and hydroponic marijuana, and creators of stained-glass lamps or Breton bagpipes. Out there were people who lived in the barn or built themselves geodesic domes. They kept bees. They drove backroad vehicles with no licence plates. They played the flute naked in the woods. Knowing that the Paradis family came from the south shore, but also that they had a lumber business there, did help to bring Russell Paradis into perspective. A lumber business was very straight but he was the artistic one. That would be why the extended family was here to celebrate the launching of *Atermoiements*. He was their one eccentric member and now they were waiting for him to read. The noise was levelling off.

Denis, on the other hand, still at his post behind the cash box, had had more beer and was becoming almost expansive, for Denis. When Marc-André came back to the table and sat down with him, he smiled that tight smile and offered one of his cheroots, which Marc-André accepted.

'Selling many books?' Marc-André asked him.

Denis held out a lighted match. For a moment he said nothing. But the reading still hadn't started, so he spoke.

'Yes, they're selling. You sell a poetry book at the launch or not at all. Because after that everyone forgets about it. After that only libraries buy it, so their collections will be complete, or else to fill up their budgets, I don't know, and reviewers buy it who want to dump on it because they didn't get a free copy, and members of the family buy it to give to other members of the family at Christmas time. After he's signed it of course. Not many read it though. Doesn't matter. Anyway, you know all that.'

And it didn't matter, because now that the door had stopped banging open and shut, Russell was preparing to read great swatches of the book to the assembled multitude himself. The sound system was turned off and the espresso machine silenced. The Radio-Canada team moved into position between a pair of pillars. Conversations petered out. The last person to realize that it was time to stop talking was Shawna from Newfoundland, who was being introduced to dry martinis by Pierre. He must have moved their conversation on to more human subjects than tides and icebergs, because Shawna was flushed and giggling. After weeks of French immersion, the luxury of speaking English, in combination with the gin in the martinis, had cracked open the shell of her inhibitions, linguistic or other.

'NEVER in Newfoundland...!' she was shrieking, then realized that everyone else was silent. 'Oh, sorry,' she said and clapped her hand over her mouth.

The two big Paradis cousins had been standing at ease, but now came to attention and moved across from the bar. It was true that they looked a little like Russell himself, tall, heavy and broad-shouldered. The difference between the poet and his cousins was largely a matter of style, length of hair, clothing, and to a certain extent facial expression. They were impassive, Russell wasn't. Yet he would probably have played hockey with them a few years ago. And these two would still be playing hockey a couple of nights a week. Tonight was an exception. Tonight they were doing their family duty by accompanying their aunt, so inexplicably husbandless, to this cultural event. Just by being here, just by standing solidly at ease, filling up space and observing the event with such admirable aloofness, they were backing their cousin the poet, lending him their support. *Faire acte de présence*, that was what they were doing, their mere presence being a generous contribution to the success of his launch, since they didn't look likely to read any sort of book and certainly not poetry. In a confidential undertone, one of them was telling the other a succinct story.

'My four-wheel-drive Silverado, you know?'

'Yeah.'

While Megan, a little at a loss when she found herself abandoned by her friend Shawna, and looking for a place to see better, squeezed herself between them. After all they had been talking to her at the bar, before Pierre interposed himself, and her French was better than Shawna's. The two men shifted slightly apart but went on conferring with each other.

'Well, my daughter, you know my girl, she rolled it ...'

'You mean the truck?'

'Yeah. Flipped it right over.'

'That's bad,' said the other man, the bald one. 'She hurt?'

Now Megan was able to see but had no place to set her beer down. Over her head, the exchange continued.

'Not really. Shaken up. Messed up the truck though.'

The bald man moved uneasily as Megan, transferring her glass from one hand to the other, elbowed him in the wallet. He put his hand on it. One had to be careful in these crowded places.

'Insurance?' he asked.

'She's too young, wasn't supposed to be driving it.'

Megan wasn't following this exchange because their French was too simple for her. She could understand fairly well when she knew what people were talking about, or could at least identify syntactical forms, but this was rudimentary, almost monosyllabic, and therefore opaque. Anyway, if these guys didn't want to talk to her, well then, right, she was concentrating on Russell as he stood off to the side of the microphone and turned the pages of his book, choosing something to read. This was art and therefore part of the immersion she had paid for, so she was determined to profit from it.

'So what'd you do, tell them you were driving?'

'Not quite. Told them it was my wife driving.'

'Smart.'

'But then they wanted to know what she was doing ice-fishing by herself at four in the morning.'

'She was by herself?'

'My wife? She was with me ...'

'No, no, your daughter.'

'Oh. No. Not really ...'

'Boyfriend...?'

'Guess so.'

'Could be complicated ...'

The Silverado man shrugged.

Then a pianist, presumably another member of the Paradis family, sat down at the electric piano at the far end of the room and started into some bluesy-sounding music.

And settling into her spot, Megan inadvertently leaned against the man with the daughter and the Silverado.

'Oops, sorry ...' she said when he moved away. 'I thought you was a pillar...!'

The man pretended he hadn't heard or didn't understand. He and his buddy traded glances.

Two of Denis's other house poets made their way to the table nearest the microphone, nodding to Madame Paradis as they passed her. They sat down, looking serious, ignoring the tribalism of the event. When their books were published, they'd do the same thing, invite all their aunts and uncles. They knew the routine.

The music stopped. A French literature professor from a south shore Cégep stepped up to the microphone to introduce the poet, while Raymonde continued to circulate through the crowd, now offering a tray with chunks of cheese on toothpicks and little greasy slices of pâté. With their mouths full, people offered her their congratulations. She smiled and moved on.

'C'est trop,' said Marc-André from the book table, narrowing his eyes at the sight of the Cégep professor.

He couldn't bear it. He tried to tell Denis that the literature professor had recently published a list of articles gleaned from three nineteenth-century Québec newspapers. He had ferreted out all references to the log drive and counted and collated the number of times it was called *la drave.*

'That was the entire content of his work, that was it!' Marc-André was saying.

'Shhhh ...' said Denis.

At last the crowd was fully silent. The professor was beginning to speak in a rich, plummy French. He compared Russell to Rimbaud, not mentioning that Rimbaud had written his great work when he was more than twenty years younger than this pink-headed, artificially youthful man, politely standing back two paces, smiling and waiting to read. Then the professor went on to compare him to Baudelaire, carefully skirting any direct references to Baudelaire's personal life or quotations from his work, for the sake of the family members present. *'Baudelaire...!'* Marc-André said Denis, in a semi-suppressed snort, 'Baudelaire would have eaten him for breakfast ...'

'Hmm. Maybe. You really think that Baudelaire ate breakfast...?'

Denis settled back with his beer. Marc-André finished the cheroot and moved quietly off through the people. He was looking for Raymonde again.

By this time the professor was comparing Russell to Émile

Nelligan, not mentioning the latter's schizophrenia, or his melancholy end in an institution, middle-aged and humble and confused. But he'd gone into too much detail and, seeing that people were beginning to fidget, he quickly left off any further speculations about Russell's artistic precursors and stood aside to let the creator read.

Russell Paradis did read very well. In fact he read better than he wrote, giving his workmanlike hermeticism a rich significance that it did not quite achieve on the page. He was perhaps a better actor than he was a poet. There was a genuine hush as his voice rolled out through the room and his listeners relaxed and soaked it up. The words didn't mean very much but they sounded as if they might, full of sensuous inflections and suggestive word combinations. Lots of symbols were in there too: flowing water, vegetation sprouting, the roots of things, then their uprooting. Tendrils. Fire. Ice. Mythic animals of course, and suggestions of breakage and tearing away.

'*Le sexe, évidemment,*' said Marc-André to Raymonde, in her ear. He'd found her and come up behind her.

She looked wearily at him.

'Shusshhhh...!'

Her wrist was getting tired and she set her tray down on one of the tall tables.

Now Russell was piling up a long string of sonorous nouns, climaxing with an explosive verb before moving on into a counterpoint of self-critical reflections, a litany of humiliation, despair and dashed hopes. He was holding nothing back, peeling open the thick pink skin of his psyche to show the throbbing organs within. In nicely calculated stages, he allowed them to glimpse the dawn of hope and the daybreak of revelation, followed all too quickly by the appearance of the shadow, then of the abyss. It was intimate, they were all his intimates, his closest confidants, and he was showing them that he *knew* they were aware of this. And they did know, everyone

33

understood, the barriers were down (or so it seemed) and they could believe that he would understand them too.

He became more specific. He moved on into suggestions of all the comforting internal intricacies of an unnamed lady whom he loved, while Raymonde stood looking steadily down at the sparkly bows on the points of her shoes and Marc-André moved off again, almost as if he actually wanted to avoid embarrassing her. He went back to Denis, looking for another smoke. But Russell's relations had no such scruples. They studied her. The long succession of Russell's girlfriends must be known to quite a few people here. Some of them probably admired Raymonde because she'd lasted for a whole three years. Of course she knew that they were assessing her. Usually she was on the alert, her stance that familiar attitude of expectation and readiness, combined with a hint of defensiveness. But now she was submissive. This was a different part of her role. Enduring the poems was her job too, and just as important as passing out food or kissing people at the door.

She even tried to look as if she liked it. Yes, her demure attitude seemed to announce, here I am, pleased and proud to be the chosen one of this great man. And who would have guessed that I was such a firecracker in bed?

It was most unlikely that any of Russell's other – or former – girlfriends were in the room, although Raymonde couldn't be sure. She was almost certain of being the only woman there who knew what Russell Paradis was like in bed, knew how clinically skilful yet how strangely cold he was about sex. Raymonde could certainly never have described to anyone how impassively he performed, interested yet detached. She was thankful that the poems concealed at least that part. Surely there was no one here who could ever suspect what she knew, how he participated in coitus without seeming to enjoy it.

It was at that moment, however, while she waited there, studying the bows on her shoes, that the tension which had been inhabiting her ever since the door began banging open and shut suddenly convulsed and gave birth to an idea. All at once, and quite unexpectedly, Raymonde understood what it was about Russell. He was a voyeur. He's always taking notes, she realized, it's not inspiration, he's just methodically taking notes.

Meanwhile the family could make their own observations. What they must have seen was a weary woman, looking perhaps a little older than Russell – although about that they would have been wrong – with her dyed hair showing brittle under the shaft of a spotlight and her skin looking not quite firm enough to carry its present load of make-up. Even observing these flaws, however, the family liked and accepted her because she put up with Russell and because she was willing to endure the poems.

By this time even Denis was studying her. Marc-André, sighting along the line of his gaze, wondered exactly how he saw her. Then Russell had come to a pause in his reading and was smiling into the lights, to an uneven scatter of applause. People with glasses in their hands were having difficulty clapping and a certain amount of wine was slopped. Food fell to the floor. The blues piano resumed, providing cover for conversation, and Marc-André turned to Denis.

'What's she doing with him?' he asked. 'She's a nice normal woman. What does he need her for?'

Denis inhaled deeply and continued looking at her.

'She does her job,' he said, 'and she does it well.'

'They both do that,' said Marc-André.

'And that's what he needs her for.'

'How old would you say she is?'

This was the sort of information that Denis was supposed to possess. He held his cigarillo over the ashtray, thoughtfully baring his teeth.

'Forty, a bit more ...' he said, finally.

'With no children, no ex-husbands ...'

'Not that I've heard of.'

'She's not bad looking,' said Marc-André.

Denis carefully turned the ash of his cigarillo against the side of the ashtray, not breaking off too much of it. He stuck it back in his mouth and spoke around it.

'No,' he said, 'but she's short and ... not thin exactly, sort of stiff. Plus her head's too big.'

'He'll never marry her,' said Marc-André, 'does she know that? Wonder if she knows what *atermoiements* means.'

Denis gave a bark of laughter that might have been a cough, and was just saying something about the desirability of single-word titles when a woman behind them broke in on their conversation.

'What does that word mean anyway?'

Denis and Marc-André looked up, startled.

Laughing in a wide-eyed, artificial way, she asked, 'Did I hear you say it had something to do with *marriage?*'

Denis gave her a hard stare. If he knew what the word *atermoiements* meant he wasn't going to share it with her. Although he hadn't shifted a millimetre, his body language had changed, his laid-back pose no longer relaxed but simply immobile. Without moving, he managed to communicate an unwillingness to have anything to do with the woman. Let her think that knowing what titles meant wasn't part of his job description.

Marc-André, however, turned on her without hesitation.

'*Bonsoir, Madame,*' he said, 'allow me to introduce myself. My name is Octave Crémazie.'

And he leapt up, seized her hand, bent over it and kissed it with much nuzzling.

'*Atermoiements.* I can explain it for you. First of all, it means all the delaying arrangements that are dragged out when you owe someone something and are not in a hurry to pay. And then it can mean the same thing but on an extended metaphorical level, procrastination and tergiversation and so on. Putting things off. Never let it be said that Octave Crémazie left a poetry-loving lady in need of enlightenment ...'

The woman didn't quite pull her hand away. She stared at Marc-André, smiling fixedly but hesitating too, seemingly less interested in his explanation than in the fact that he had kissed her hand. Denis, off the hook, smoked and watched her struggling with the situation. She was clearly troubled by the name as well, because she did recognize it. She knew that she'd heard it before, but where? Assailed by uncertainty, she gave another nervous laugh. Octave? Did she know an Octave? Was she supposed to know an Octave? Her smile froze into a grimace of doubt, then resentment, as she suspected mockery. She snatched her hand away and turned her back. Marc-André smirked at Denis.

'She's not stupid, you know ...'

'Who, that one? Let me tell you ...'

'No, no, Raymonde ...'

Denis shrugged and stretched his lips into a smile, neatly exposing his teeth and a smoky exhalation, like a visible sign of impatience. Marc-André was about to pursue his line of questioning when the pianist reached a final chord. The intermission was over. Russell stepped up to the microphone again and the woman Marc-André had embarrassed wheeled around to look over her shoulder at him. She was too far off to hear what he was saying, but her stare was angry enough to silence him at least for the conclusion of Russell's reading.

Denis sat through the rest of it with his head back and his eyes half-closed, his hands in his pockets, breathing out clouds of blue smoke, some of it in rings that drifted down around his ears. Although he looked oblivious, he was still guarding the books and keeping an eye on the door. And Russell was finishing his last ode to the unnamed girlfriend, letting them all know that she was his solace and his inspiration and the mother of his thought, although his biological mother was also present, if not actually listening to him.

In fact there was a minor disturbance happening at her table. Madame Paradis was being regaled, in a piercing whisper, by the woman who had failed to remember if she knew an Octave or not. Then the whisper evolved into a louder tone, almost a shriek. She was telling Madame something about an operation. *La grande opération.* She seemed to be a little unstable. Madame Paradis was listening with pained politeness.

'Ben oui,' she said, not too discreetly, 'que voulez-vous? Ces choses-là arrivent de temps à autre. Il faut passer par là.'

Madame made it sound as if anyone might need a hysterectomy and she herself had had several. Nothing to it.

Russell could hear this exchange perfectly but did not look at either of the women. He began to distribute thanks. He thanked his parents for their encouragement and support over the past thirty-five years. Madame Paradis must have taken this as a signal because now, still sitting on her chair, she was pulling her parka up around her shoulders. While Russell thanked the Zénob for the platters of cheese and pâté and crackers, she'd got the parka on and was arranging it over the layers of her skirt.

Marc-André looked at Denis.

'I thought you paid for the food.'

Denis blew another smoke ring. The poet never knew who paid for what. That was typical of poets. Russell was thanking all the friends who had displayed their commitment to literature by coming out here this evening and standing around and buying the book, and he fulsomely thanked the pianist, who did indeed turn out to be a brother-in-law, as one artist to another. His mother stood up and barged out through the crowd, which parted before her. Her passage made a difference.

The packed mass of poetry-lovers was loosening at the centre. The man with the daughter and the Silverado slid quietly out after her.

'Got to see how far up the water is,' he said, to no one in particular, and headed for the door. Megan moved into the space where he'd been standing.

Russell was once again thanking the woman who was his light, his love, his centre and his soul, while Raymonde continued to stare unhappily at her shoes. Thus she didn't notice as Madame Paradis passed her with a simple nod. Finally Russell thanked Denis, who was at that moment selling a copy of *Atermoiements* to the Silverado man. He'd come in before the book table was set up, but he didn't succeed in getting past Denis on the way out. The bald man did escape, however, and the two of them escorted Madame Paradis up the steps and out.

'She left in a hurry,' said someone.

'Getting away from that hysterical woman,' said someone else.

But it was more likely that the mother of the poet was simply going home, her job done and acknowledged. When Raymonde did look up and glimpse a vanishing flounce of skirt between the two cousins and the metal strip across the bottom of the door, she was glad to see the last of her. Meanwhile Russell was thanking the designer and the printer of the book, and the Cégep professor, although he had also left, possibly by the back door, since no one had seen him go, and the Zénob all over again for providing the space. Then last of all – and Russell rolled this out with a flourish and a pause, during which the espresso machine went back to its work, producing a long-drawn-out gagging sound – he deepened his voice, cleared his throat and offered his thanks to the Muse.

At the other end of the room Denis, counting the take, bit off a smoke ring with another bark of laughter and winced through it. The cameraman lowered his camera from his

shoulder and left. One of the waiters began to circulate the
platters again although all the pâté and most of the better
cheese had been eaten. Shawna took a foil-wrapped wedge of
industrial cheese and found that the foil could no longer be
peeled off it. The cheese turned to goo in her fingers. In her
efforts, she dropped it, made a half-hearted effort at retrieving
it, and then gave up as someone stepped into it. People were
edging towards the exit and digging through the pile for their
coats. The door at the top of the steps was once more opening
and shutting as they left.

'*Voilà, une nation d'épiciers,*' said Marc-André as the last of
the tinfoil cheese wedges went past. 'Who said that?'

'Octave Crémazie,' said Denis, promptly. He'd worked for
the Ministère des Affaires culturelles. He knew his stuff.

'Right,' said Marc-André, 'a nation of grocers ...' and he
glared across at the hysterectomy woman, who had heard him
and was looking angrily at both of them.

Denis avoided looking back at her.

'Listen ...' he said to Marc-André.

But there was a jostling and an outcry from the door. Someone, leaving, had slipped and fallen *up* the steps. It was
Shawna, now tittering helplessly as Pierre picked her up.

'Well, maybe sometimes, but NEVER in Newfoundland...!'
she was insisting.

Pierre helped her out the door while Marc-André left Denis
and walked across to Russell. His performance over, he'd gone
straight back to his circle of acolytes. One of them had ordered
him another Armagnac and he was already surrounded by
young men telling him that they knew just what he meant.
Really drunk now, not only with the alcohol but also with the
sound of his own voice, he was once more talking intently, passionately, to the bunch of people by the washroom door. He was
warm and excited, carried on the wave of words and feeling that
he had created, and wanting to give of himself and his ideas.

'*La sensualisation, voire le sensuel ...*' he was saying.

His admirers surrounded him, hanging on his words, while the departures continued.

'*Et la rupture ... briser le silence ... l'aventure de la pudeur tacite ... tactile ... la fille et le ...*'

Soon the room was almost clear. The hysterectomy woman snatched up her coat and rushed away up the steps. The door banged hard behind her. Even the regulars at the back were down to two, conferring over their beer. But Russell was talking ever more intently.

'*Le débâcle ... et la CHUTE ...*'

'*Cute,*' said Marc-André, heading over to the bar.

There he found the plumbing wholesaler, who was now sitting next to the blond telephone systems processor and staring intently, gloomily at her.

Avoiding that tête-à-tête, he settled in at the far end by the kitchen door. The two regulars still there turned out to be making bets on how much longer it would take the plumbing parts man to be processed. Marc-André turned his back to them and watched Raymonde from there. She'd faithfully returned to the foot of the steps and was still smiling bravely as she saw people out the door.

Even the circle around Russell was thinning. There was only one counter-current to the movement of departures. Although Shawna and her tides man were gone, the inscrutable cameraman was back. He'd returned without his camera and had installed himself at the other end of the bar. There he was chatting up Megan, whose French was more and more functional. Marc-André wasn't close enough to hear them. It was Raymonde, from her post by the door, who was treated to a fresh rendition of the usual political discussion. Had the cameraman made some remark about English Canada? Megan was spluttering desperately, trying to get across to him that she'd never even *been* there. She was from Newfoundland and Canada was *away*. He smiled ironically at her, watching her mouth move.

'*Nous sommes la AUTRE society distincte...!*' she quavered, apparently trying not to weep.

Why did no one understand? Newfoundland was a nation. Patiently, the cameraman reached over and took her wrist in both his hands to show her that he did understand.

Raymonde tried to ignore the pair of them. The language exchange students were, in the very great majority, women. They made the effort, they took the risk, and year after year they came to Québec and went through this. The French lover. Most men, English or French-speaking, stayed home where they could speak the language they were used to, the language in which they were equipped to take advantage. She moved into the centre of the room, looking vaguely around for something to do, someone to kiss, and suddenly found herself in a black patch of emptiness. Why was she even here? Why did she exist? What was the point of all this vapid seduction, repeated over and over again? With Russell at the back, talking to a circle of young men.

Alphonse Piché was standing at the bar with his grey wool coat on, trying not to watch as the cameraman worked at seducing Megan, but also holding out money to pay. Raymonde went over to him.

'Are you okay, Alphonse, do you need a ride home?'

She had no car, but for Alphonse, she would have collared someone.

'I'm fine, *chère*, I've got a lift coming. We're supposed to be going out to dinner with ... thingamajig.' Names could be a problem for Alphonse. 'But who was that woman?'

'What woman?'

Raymonde wondered if he meant the hysterical woman, who had left. She turned around and looked at Megan, but that wasn't where Alphonse was looking. Besides, Megan was holding hands with the Radio-Canada man.

'You don't mean that one who wanted to make a fuss about her operation...?'

Alphonse straightened his shoulders. He looked pityingly at Raymonde.

'*Non, ma chère,* I do not. Although maybe you should know that that woman was in fact an old girlfriend of Russell's ...'

Raymonde felt the black emptiness rise up and wrap itself completely around her.

'... but I'm talking about the woman who kissed me, earlier on. You were there, you spoke to me. You saw her. She *really* kissed me.'

Raymonde heard him but couldn't deal with what he wanted.

'Oh ... I don't know her name, Alphonse ...'

And she turned away, trying to breathe calmly, trying to see through the blackness. What she saw was Denis putting the remaining copies of *Atermoiements* back into the cardboard box on the floor under the table. Why hadn't he told her? Denis always knew that sort of thing. He dropped the cash box in on top and closed the flaps. That was what the scene with Madame Paradis had been all about. But Denis could have warned her. Now he was swallowing the last of his beer. He set the empty glass down and tilted his chair back on two legs again, finishing his cheroot. He blew one final, perfect smoke ring, which this time twisted and writhed upwards, its convolutions opening and gently spreading like a slow furry grey flower. Denis watched it go. He observed as it was sucked into a ceiling vent. Then he pulled the box of books and money out from under the table, stood up, and carried it all away, up the steps and out into the night. He didn't have a coat and left just as he was, in his eternal suit.

From her black hole amidst the chairs and tables, Raymonde watched as, arm in arm, Megan and the cameraman went up the steps behind Denis and also vanished into the night. After them went the blond woman, resolutely followed by the plumbing parts man. And then Alphonse left, stooping forward to climb the steps alone, in a posture of resignation.

But if that was what Raymonde saw, Marc-André, from the back of the room, instead saw one of Russell's young men come in through the passage from the rear exit, closed now because it was getting cold, take two coats from the coat rack and, quickly turning his back to the room, go out that way without looking at anyone. Marc-André wheeled around from that discovery in time to observe Raymonde looking up the steps after Alphonse, her face set in sadness. She looked lost. Moving mechanically, she bent and gathered up her handbag from under the book table. She slung that on her shoulder. Then she collected her coat from the table behind her, where there was no longer any heap. She seemed to be looking nowhere. And Russell was nowhere in sight.

Immediately it was all very clear to Marc-André, as Raymonde moved helplessly towards the back. At some point in the last few minutes Russell must have gone out that way, stepped out for some fresh air, or to talk to someone privately, or – when the toilets were all occupied – to relieve himself in the snow. Raymonde hadn't even put her coat on, but held it bundled against herself as she headed for the back door. Marc-André slid off his barstool and followed, plucking his parka from a hook as he passed it in the little corridor. He shrugged himself into it while Raymonde pushed at the door, opening it into the night. Both of them had forgotten about the wind, which yanked the door out of her hands. Marc-André came up behind her just as she let it go and stepped out after it.

Although it was dark, it was hardly cold out there. Masses of damp air were battering against the building and whooping up into the night sky. There was a life-giving excitement to the wet translucent gleam of sodium vapour light in the sky behind the black house shapes. And for a moment, the wind was good.

Raymonde stumbled over the case of empty beer bottles that must have been used, earlier, to prop the door open, and thus was saved from stepping into the pool of vomit in the little concrete well at the bottom of the outdoor steps. It had taken her a moment to smell it. Then a down draft brought it to her. She recoiled. Marc-André was right behind her and smelled it at almost the same moment. Russell wasn't there but someone had been sick in the areaway. A long string of vomit descended the snowbank and formed a puddle just beside Raymonde's shoe. When she stepped quickly back, still clutching her rolled-up coat, she tripped against the beer case again and fell into Marc-André's arms.

'Puis-je vous aider, Madame...?'

When she ignored his irony and said nothing, he drew her back into the opening of the door.

'Is he out there?' he asked, knowing perfectly well that there was no one.

Raymonde let him hold her for ten or fifteen seconds. She swallowed hard.

'No,' she said, finally, in a careful voice, 'but I think some-one's been sick out here ...'

'Yes, that's obvious. Well, does it stink of Armagnac? Because that would be our friend Russell.'

Raymonde looked very, very tired. She wiped the side of her shoe, carefully, in the crunchy snow by the door jamb, even though there was nothing on it. She shrank sideways, out of Marc-André's arms, and stepped past him, back inside. When he took her coat out of her hands, however, she let him help her into it.

'I guess he just wasn't feeling well enough to stay. He must have gone home.'

Although she was trying hard to control her face, her mouth trembled. After all her efforts, Russell hadn't bothered to talk to anyone but his cronies. And then he'd got puking drunk and left without so much as telling her. She stood uncertainly by the row of barstools along the back wall. To look busy, she gathered up some glasses and carried them to the bar, where Marc-André had left his copy of *Atermoiements*. The last two regular drinkers had gone and the book was lying alone on the Formica surface. She pushed the glasses across the bar as he gathered it up.

'Did he sign it for you?' she asked, looking across at the thing in his hands.

'Yes,' he said, shoving it into his pocket. 'Come on.'

'Did he write anything else in it? What did he say?'

There was a note of insistence in her voice, almost like the beginning of anger.

'I'll show you. But come on. Do up your coat.'

She did up a couple of buttons and stopped, as if trying to remember something. What had she not done? While she wavered, Marc-André seized her arm with his sinewy hand. He was as tall as she was, or almost, and he escorted her up the steps and out to the rue Bonaventure.

There they found Alphonse Piché, still waiting on the sidewalk for his ride to supper.

'*Re-bonsoir, les enfants,*' he said.

He looked wisely at the two of them and Raymonde became self-conscious about Marc-André's hand on her arm. She pulled away from him.

'Oh, Alphonse, have you seen Russell? We don't know where he went ...'

'No, *chère*, I haven't. He didn't go past this way. But did you find out who that woman was?'

'Woman ...' said Marc-André.

He took a firmer grip on Raymonde's arm.

'The tall one with the red hair, the one who kissed me, earlier on.'

Raymonde stood away from Marc-André and took a deep

breath. The change of subject, plus the chance to be helpful, restored some of her aplomb.

'I know who he means,' she said. 'I saw her kiss him. But I just don't know her name. It was the woman from Radio-Canada. The one who had the cameraman with her. They were filming Russell.'

'Let me tell you,' said Alphonse, 'that woman knows how to kiss. I want to know what her name is.'

'You can ask Denis,' said Marc-André. 'He knows all the public relations stuff. But tomorrow. He's gone now. So tomorrow. We won't forget. Find out name of kissing lady for Alphonse.'

'Elle embrassait vraiment, cette femme,' Alphonse said, with dignity, 'that woman knew how to kiss.'

And he stared sadly up the street towards the cathedral, perhaps because he was expecting his ride to arrive from that direction. From his pedestal across the street, the statue of Duplessis looked down on the three of them. In his day, the Zénob had been a private house, and the basement had been used for parties by the children of the comfortable bourgeoisie. But Alphonse, looking up the street, remained unaware of him.

'C'est vite fait, la vie,' he said, simply. Life is soon over.

Raymonde and Marc-André looked at each other. Before either of them could try to answer him, Alphonse left them and walked away up the street in the direction of the rue Hart. They saw the wind lift his white hair, which shone under the streetlights. Before he reached the cross street, a car passed them, overtook him, slowed alongside and stopped. Someone they couldn't see got out to hold the door and help him in.

Then they both turned into the wind and walked the other way, across Notre-Dame and down towards the river. The monument outside the post office, which sometimes had a flame flaring from the top of it, was dark.

'Is this where you're parked?' asked Raymonde.

'Right there,' said Marc-André, jerking his elbow at a small muddy car, 'but come on, let's go and take a look at the river.'

They walked on down to the Terrasse Turcotte, which overlooks the river, and picked their way through drooling heaps of snow to the railing at the edge. Marc-André looked down at Raymonde's patent-leather shoes.

'Didn't you have boots?'

'Yes, but ...'

'You left them back in the Zénob.'

'They were under the table. I forgot them.'

'Never mind, we'll walk in the bare spots.'

He let go of her arm and held out his hand but she stepped away from him and made her own way over the frozen places between the puddles to the railing. Below them, the water was a moving mass of ice floes shoving past, not just in the channel like winter ice, but right across the breadth of the river. Lac Saint-Pierre was breaking up and its whole surface was moving downstream. The glinting floes were also thinner than winter ice and not so white, riding low and glassy on the swelling current, only clearly visible at points where lights from the promenade struck the water. Closer in was a wash of frozen debris, broken and slushy. This served to show, even through the dark, how fast the water was rising, swelling up over the edge of the port below them.

In the summer, crowds of people strolled along down there, enjoying the cool breeze from the river and gawking into the cruise boat from Kingston, but tonight even the coast guard ship had cast off and was standing out in the channel, chugging against the current and belching greasy exhaust into the clean wind. The lower level of the promenade was awash with thick grey water and cordoned off with yellow plastic tape. Raymonde held her coat collar up and faced upstream into the wind.

'So is this the tide going out now or is it already coming back in...?'

Marc-André stood close beside her but without touching her.

'There's not enough tide in Trois-Rivières to make any difference. And I have no idea whether it's coming in or going out. You mean what Pierre Arcand said? Back in the Zénob? He was just talking. He doesn't know either. This is high water, this is a flood. It's spring.'

'Spring.'

Raymonde wrapped her arms around herself and stared out at the faint lights of Sainte-Angèle-de-Laval on the south shore, that other world. When Marc-André pulled his copy of *Atermoiements* out of his coat pocket, she held out her hand for it.

'Now let me see what he wrote in it for you ...'

But he held it out of reach.

'Nothing much,' he said. 'You couldn't read it in this light anyway.'

'Well, let me try, you said you'd let me look at it.'

'It's nothing special really, just the usual stuff about being comrades in art, some garbage like that ...'

'You're too hard on him,' said Raymonde. 'You don't give him credit for anything. Talking about the shape of his head ...'

'Why are you defending him? He's gone off God knows where with some of his boyfriends and all you get from him is a pile of puke in the snow.'

'You're unfair, oh, you're unfair. He was sick. He'll be home tonight.'

'He'll be home when it's convenient for him, when he needs sleep or food or clean clothes.'

Raymonde faced the river and said nothing.

'And you know that,' Marc-André insisted. 'You know perfectly well that he's using you. He's used others before you. Why should I have to tell you what you already know?'

He put the book back into his pocket while Raymonde thought of that other, hysterical woman and shuddered. She continued to gaze out at the procession of broken ice jostling past in the dark river. At least the wind was helping her to feel better. Maybe Denis had been right after all not to tell her who the frantic woman was. Certainly it was better if Marc-André didn't have that information at his disposal. Russell had called him facile. Would he say something facile about that – if he knew? She didn't want to give him the chance. Other things were more important. Even the ice floes were more important, with their pressure, their urgency, the way they kept coming, an endless parade travelling, travelling. She looked down into the moving mass.

'Just keeps pushing and pushing,' she said, 'in such a big hurry, as if they had some reason. All the different broken pieces, as if they were really coming from somewhere and needed to be somewhere else. But where are they going?'

Marc-André shoved his hands into his pockets and encountered Russell's book. He brought it out again.

'Out to sea is where they're going, Raymonde,' he said – and she noticed that at last he'd dropped the sarcastic mannerism of calling her *Madame* – 'and as you know, it's all coming down from Lac Saint-Pierre. But you need meaning too…? Well, all right, if that's what you want, I can give you meaning. It means that life is passing you by. Just watch this.'

With a flick of his wrist, he sent his copy of *Atermoiements* skimming out into the river.

'*Ah…!*'

Raymonde bent over the wet railing and strained to see the book. She knew that there had been exactly five hundred copies printed the week before. Now there were four hundred and ninety-nine. She leaned outwards to the dark water and pale ice. Swirling, bulging as if being forced by some pressure from below, the flood caught at the pale rectangle of Russell

Paradis's book. But *Atermoiements* didn't sink. It plunged in and then it was borne up. It bobbed and turned, at first revolving as it was carried outwards, then momentarily back, then outwards again to the deeper water. Raymonde saw it settle, fit itself in and go with the rest of the cold debris. The pale spot that was the book had found its place in the racing ice pack and then it was out of sight, travelling fast towards the salt water downstream. There was no point in trying to follow it. It was gone. With a little gasp, she bent her face towards her hands on the cold railing.

'You shouldn't have done that,' she said.

'No? But it was a pleasure just the same. You can tell your boyfriend that his book gave me pleasure.'

'I won't tell him at all.'

'That's what I want to hear,' said Marc-André. 'Now come and have supper with me.'

He held out his hand. Raymonde stood stiffly back, trying to make up her mind. The dizzying damp wind wasn't even cold and yet she was shivering hard. Maybe it was the strange tension that had been with her all evening. Or maybe it was just because her feet were wet. She looked down at the bows on her shoes, which no longer sparkled. And seeing that they were ruined, she remembered that Russell Paradis was a cold-hearted, exploitive voyeur.

'Come on,' said Marc-André.

Raymonde turned away from the railing. Russell's book was gone. Whatever he had written in it for Marc-André was also gone. Now there was nothing out there but the inexorable ice. So she took Marc-André's hand and went with him, not because of the black horror that had descended upon her in the Zénob, which seemed to have lifted now, and not entirely because of that tight feeling in her chest, which was still with her, and certainly not because she thought that she should. In fact she was reasonably sure that she was making a mistake. But Raymonde went with Marc-André because she did know that life was passing her by, and also because she couldn't forget the warm animal sensation of his lips and moustache on the back of her hand.

Lucifer, Beelzebub and Satan

The evening breeze, little more than the faintest motion of the dark air, lifted from the east and brought with it a hint of pulp-mill stink. The odour mingled with smells of damp ground and old wood and the early vegetation of spring. Simon inhaled it. He was snuffing it up, testing it. Hidden among the pale young leaves, that only this week had grown dense enough to conceal him, he was crouching under and against the leaning bulk of an ancient cement retaining wall. He was singing:

Freude schöner Götterfunken,
Tochter aus Elysium ...

He did think that he was singing quietly but his voice had natural depth and resonance. The sound carried, and if so far no passerby had noticed him in his lair, it was only because no one had yet gone by on the street. He was also repeating the same phrase over and over again. At one time he must have set out to learn the German words from the back of the record jacket but now he couldn't get beyond the daughter of Elysium. Breathing deeply, he rolled his head against the cool, gritty cement and sang it again. Joy, creation of the gods. He hummed the melody of the next phrase, waiting for more of the lyrics to come to him. They didn't. He was stuck on the Elysium.

Tonight his own private version of Elysium had claimed him. This was because he was a week, maybe even a little more than a week, overdue for his Modecate injection. With the coming of spring and the softer weather, hoping against hope, deciding that surely he must be better by now, he'd skipped his appointment at the psychiatric clinic. Since they had no idea where he was, he was free. And for a while his optimism had carried him along. Then this evening, feeling a compelling need for the company of people, he'd gone out to the Zénob. And there, seeing everyone else drinking, he'd had a couple of beers. He'd been wanting one for a long time and ordering beer had seemed the easiest way to fit in. It was simply not reasonable that he should be unable to drink any alcohol at all. Anyone could have a beer.

For Simon, however, the two beers that he had drunk were more than enough to break his hold on everyday reality. He was supposed to know that. It was a fact that he had to learn, although tonight, after the first few swallows, it hadn't seemed to matter very much. He could forget all about it just as he forgot the humiliation and the grinding stress of solitude, because quite soon interlocutors either real or hallucinatory – he wasn't always quite sure who was real and who wasn't – had gathered all around him.

Sitting at the bar, Simon had begun talking to himself, or to someone who was or wasn't beside him, or to the barman when he happened to be standing at the spot where Simon was looking. He tried to lecture everyone and no one around him on the subject of the eighteenth century, the passage to the nineteenth, and Beethoven and the poet Schiller, and his *Ode to Joy*. At one point he suddenly recalled the sad story of how Napoleon had betrayed Beethoven's belief in his revolutionary principles. He began to lose his temper. He strayed into disconnected, aggressive lamentations about the various misplaced idealisms which are the legacy of that self-assured period in human history and forgot about Napoleon, although he was still angry. He jerked his arms in violent, impulsive gestures that might have meant something in some other context. Sitting at the bar in the Zénob, having a drink by himself, talking to himself, they meant nothing. Or they meant that he was mad.

'*Le romantisme* ...' he growled derisively into the smoke, and hung his head. Romanticism had disappointed him. Then suddenly, startlingly, he roared, 'MERDE!!' and knocked over a glass, not his own, that someone had left too close to him on the bar.

Of course none of the muscular, hair-gelled young drinkers in the Zénob had the faintest idea what was wrong with him. At first they laughed. They thought he was a joke. Then they came to see that there was something seriously disturbing about him. He was talking *insistently* to someone who really wasn't there, and even in that crowded bar, even among those sophisticated readers of Nietzsche and Louis Hamelin and Woody Allen, they gave him plenty of room. It wasn't funny after all and soon there was an empty stool on either side of him as he continued to converse with unseen companions, completely unaware of the fright he was creating in the real people around him.

Madness might be interesting as a subject for literature or philosophy or even humour, but a real crazy, they were discovering, was not reachable in any way. Not only was he becoming more and more alarming, he was also tiresome. After all, he was totally wrapped up in his own bizarre world. He was incapable of taking a coherent interest in anyone else around him.

Equally oblivious of the recorded bar music or, in its turn, of the electric piano, finally Simon had opened up and launched into the chorus from Beethoven's Ninth Symphony.

'*Freude schöner Götterfunken* ...'

His powerful voice, perfectly in tune, could be heard, easily, over all the other noise.

'*Tochter aus Elysium...!*'

And if he could have got any further, they might even have listened for a while. But not only did he repeat the phrase over and over again, he began to rock back and forth, hunched over and howling out the German words. From time to time he paused, and could be seen to be protesting, apparently to someone beside him, and resisting comments or orders that only he could hear. By the time the pair of waiters came and shoved him up the stairs and out the door, he was too confused to be entirely sure if that was really what was happening. They locked the door behind him and waited to see him go away. But he seemed to believe that he had been asked to sing and now he understood only that there was some unexpected change of programme. He was indignant. Why were they suddenly telling him not to sing, what was he supposed to think? He couldn't understand why he'd been helped outside. He couldn't figure out why the door wouldn't open again. Baffled, he tugged at the handle. There were people in there but they weren't looking at him, they didn't seem to see him. Had *he* become invisible? His voices were usually invisible. Unsure and unhappy, he wavered for a while then wandered off along the street.

And when, from inside the bar, they saw that he was gone, there were shouts of laughter. They unlocked the door again. The piano player switched off his instrument and went and found a tape of the Ninth Symphony, which they actually played for a few minutes. But it wasn't long before they went back to the blues and forgot about Simon. His passage at the Zénob was only a brief part of their evening's entertainment.

Meanwhile Simon, still lonely, still needing some contact with other people, was wandering eastward into the smaller streets. After the long winter, the mild spring air was a liberation in itself. At the intersection of Haut-Boc and Saint-François-Xavier, he came to an old red-brick trade school, L'École des Métiers, recently converted into seniors' condominiums. The breeze lifted a few long grey strands of his hair as he stared at the concrete base of the building, where some bilingual punk had spray-painted: SICK OF IT ALL. Simon did understand the English but was trying to decode its message, seeing it as the name of the building, something in the spirit of the names on retirement cottages. 'Journey's End.' 'Le Repos du guerrier.' That sort of thing.

There would be no red-brick condominium for Simon at his journey's end. He turned the corner and paused at the top of des Commissaires, looking down the slope of the street towards the paper mill, trying to decode the noise in his ears. The voices. The perceptions might be real or they could be from inside his head. He was never quite sure where his messages were coming from. There was always interference.

From this point the rumble of the paper mill could be heard and on some nights an orange glow from it could be seen in the sky above the houses. He looked down that way and saw only the moon, not quite full but huge and bulging with a baleful yellow glow as it crawled up the sky. On other nights there was a smell from the mill. At the corner of des Commissaires, with the noise in his ears turning to a high-pitched ringing, Simon began to detect that familiar sulphurous foulness.

He started slowly along the sidewalk, wheeling now and again to look behind him, smelling the air and thinking about his devils. Of course it was they who'd been urging him to sing, back there in the Zénob, but in the scuffle of his departure they'd flown away. Now he was waiting for their return. Sometimes they announced themselves with the reek of something vile, hellfire he supposed, he wasn't sure, but the pulpmill smell could certainly be brimstone. It did carry those suggestions of filth and burning. To Simon it meant that his devils were somewhere close at hand and he was glad. He was feeling the need of their diabolical support.

Then between the rue Sainte-Ursule and the rue Sainte-Angèle he'd found himself attracted, suddenly, by the secret green space he was now hiding in, a stub of laneway left over from the French Régime plan of the city, too narrow for modern traffic and this year filled with the sprouting saplings of weedy trees. Peering into the leaves, by this time Simon was actually searching for his devils, sniffing for them, looking for-ward to meeting them. He was titillated by the thought of wait-ing for them in there between two streets named for lady saints. But first he looked both ways. Rejection in the Zénob had left that much of a mark. Sick of it all. Since there was no one else on the street, no one to ask him what he was up to, he stepped in amongst the leaves and hid himself.

It was the sort of wild spot that only the slums of an old city can provide, and the perfect place to await the devils. They were under control now, or that was what Simon thought. They had become his friends and colleagues and he was glad of their presence. Hunkered down in the secret thicket, he sang for a while, then fell silent, waiting and listening. Hoping. After all he'd been singing to please them. And the ringing in his ears, like the foul odour, was another sign that they were with him, about to manifest themselves. He breathed shallowly. An elderly couple walked past, the man saying something to the woman about a lawnmower, and Simon was pleased that they hadn't seen him crouching in the bushes. He smiled with secret satisfaction and went back to sniffing the air.

Simon didn't realize how long his hair was, or how grey, and he hadn't noticed that his jean jacket was almost transparent across the shoulders, with ragged holes in the elbows. He was unaware that he was a shabby, bloated man with straggling hair and an untrimmed beard, but he had noticed that people avoided him. And the result of all this was that most of the time his devils provided the only companionship in his life. Some-times, for as much as a week, theirs were the only voices which he heard addressing him. The devils not only talked to him, they commented on his activities, they remembered things that he had forgotten. They alone understood his dreams and ambitions, and his love of music. And if they also harangued, criticized and insulted him, that was simply the price he had to pay for their attention. He was not alone. If anyone had consented to listen, Simon would have been glad to describe how Lucifer, Beelzebub and Satan were joining him for an evening's stroll through the old industrial-residential quarter of Trois-Rivières, under the plume of the paper mill.

The lane that abutted here in the greenery no longer served for the delivery of coal or wood or ice to the back doors of the houses in the two streets, but it was still used by a few bread and soft-drink trucks. Up the slope it was a functional thoroughfare. It was only this stub of it that was overgrown with the thrusting shoots of *érables à Giguère*. From the other side of the rue des Commissaires the lane wended its way northwest, uphill and away from the St Lawrence, then levelled out and went all the way to the rue Saint-Maurice and the shopping centre.

On the higher ground overhanging the uphill side of this narrowed part was a big stone house. Two hundred years back it had been the manor house for the whole area. Once it had probably overlooked fields spreading away downhill towards the St Maurice River and its confluence with the St Lawrence. Now the space that had been those fields was occupied by several streets of tenement housing, *logements* for the poor and the marginal, and at the river's edge by the paper mill. Even that was a hundred and fifty years old. But at some earlier time, maybe a century ago, maybe more, the owners of the big house had defended it with a retaining wall, which prevented its lawn from subsiding into the lower classes down the hill. It was this wall that leaned over into the lane and narrowed it. A few yards farther along, the thicket was closed off completely by a fence.

Simon remembered that the winter before last someone's old Volkswagen had spent the snowy months in here, hidden under the drifts with its tires all flat. When the spring came, and after the Volkswagen had gone the way of all metal, the tenant in the humble house on the downhill side had put up the fence and made the rest of the lane into part of his yard. That must have been illegal but the city hadn't noticed. Since then the trees had sprung up anyway, concealing everything. The stub of lane was a leafy little box canyon where Simon crouched, secure, as three young girls walked past, talking in self-absorbed voices.

Immediately his devils were with him.

'*Look at those stupid bitches*,' Satan muttered in a deep bass voice, while Lucifer tittered at the movements of their buttocks and called them vapid little twats. Beelzebub said nothing and chuckled a thoughtful baritone chuckle.

Simon, who was more interested in his familiar spirits than in the teenagers, waited until the girls were out of sight. Then he stepped out of the leaves.

He looked both ways along des Commissaires. Yes, the street was empty. On the other hand, the back of Jacqueline's flat gave onto the lane just up the slope. He wasn't thinking about her but he knew that the house where she lived was just up there and something about the season made him think of her. This was almost the beginning of summer, the first warm night at the end of May. That misshapen moon, paler now, was swelling and would be full in a night or two. Life was opening out again, as it did every year, like the wild trees, like the weeds that grew in every crack in the asphalt. Simon crossed the street and started up the lane, still feeling the urge to sing, not yet acknowledging to himself that he would also pass Jacqueline's dining-room window and her back door. He didn't need her that much. That was all finished anyway.

As he turned his back on his leafy retreat, his devils swarmed out of its darkness and flew after him. In the darkness between the sparsely placed lamp posts of the lane, the gibbous moon threw his shadow at his feet, where he and they watched it wobble and flow, trampling on it. He wiggled his fingers beside his head as he walked on his shadow, laughing, and the devils reeled and rollicked with him while the night air, still smelling of the paper mill, feathered his hair and lifted the tendrils of his beard.

Simon reasoned with himself, considering their diabolical presence. They were his best friends now, the only friends who appreciated him and encouraged him in the art of song. He was grateful for their comradeship and welcomed their different characters. Beelzebub, he had decided, represented intellectual effort, creation, music, the desire for expression and the source of the artistic impulse. Lucifer was sensuality, love, illumination, *préciosité* perhaps, maybe even homosexuality. And Satan was raw power. Cruelty. Simon was more afraid of Satan than of the other two. Satan was the one whose presence he associated with the pulpmill stink. But it seemed to him that they all strutted out ahead of him, behind him, around him, rode on his shoulder and spoke into his ear. They possessed him, in fact.

To propitiate the three of them, he sang, *'Freude schöner Götterfunken …'* and Beelzebub sang along, harmonizing perfectly, and laughed in his ear.

Was joy exclusively a creation of God? Schiller's poem seemed to say that it was. But in Simon's experience the devils had their part in it too. They were there for him when no one else was.

Happy for the moment, he strode on up the lane. Passing Jacqueline's house, he saw light and human shapes through the texture of her yellow curtains but tried not to look. There was a design of birds and fruit on the fabric and he made a conscious decision not to examine those, for fear that they might begin to swarm and change shape. Instead he continued on his way, considering the nocturnal scenery of the laneway.

He disapproved of the laundry strung across it here and there, hanging limply in the darkness, left out overnight by slovenly housekeepers who were, in his judgement, inviting theft. There were also discarded mattresses, stained and unstained, and the wreckage of some plaid-upholstered furniture, a settee and a couple of armchairs, used up now and left for the scavengers. Waste, he said to himself, foolish waste, although he knew that it was all part of the turning wheel of human activity. Some houses were neat, with everything tidied away and locked up, while others put inexplicable mounds of garbage out every night of the week, to be sorted through by humans and animals. Varieties of rickety staircases hung from the backs of three and four-storey blocks of flats, with outdoor fuel tanks propped on the balconies, cars and trucks crammed into parking spaces under them, and volunteer bushes and trees thrusting up everywhere they weren't cut back, sometimes filling entire abandoned yards. Other yards, however, were primly fenced with greenish pressure-treated wood lattices. Through these he caught glimpses of decks and sliding patio doors installed on the back kitchens of old houses. Gentrification had at least its toenail in the door, even in the rue Sainte-Angèle.

But there didn't seem to be anyone else out walking. It did not occur to Simon that people got out of the way when they saw him coming zigzagging and mumbling along the lane in the dark, and he went back again to his song, still repeating the same phrase about Joy being the daughter of Elysium. Now he was relishing the potential of his voice, the feeling of power and range, and enjoying testing its resonance against the acoustics of the lane, the volume defined by the backs of the houses. Unexpectedly, more of the words came to him.

> *Wir betreten feuertrunken,*
> *Himmlische, dein Heiligtum …*

Something about being drunk with fire and treading a holy sanctum. What he needed was a properly enclosed space, like the narrow passages between garages or the big blank back wall of a grocery store.

'*Tochter aus Elysium,*' he sang again, wanting to create an echo and feel it rolling back at him.

Satan encouraged him in this hope, told him that he was invincible, while Beelzebub, riding on his left ear, whispered that he didn't need Beethoven, that he should be writing his own stuff, he should get himself a manager, sing in the clubs, because he was wasting his talent singing in the back lanes like this, alone in the night. And Lucifer only laughed and laughed. Warmed by the interest that his devils took in him, Simon resolved that yes, he would become a songwriter. In the sound of his own voice and the static of their mutterings, he imagined the world opening before him and throwing itself at his feet. The images even became visual for a few moments and he saw Lucifer turn and smile seductively in his direction.

Then Simon gave the thought up before it was fully hatched. He would never write songs. No, no, he would simply open his throat and sing. It didn't have to be Beethoven. There were so many good songs already, so many heart-rending, heart-filling, heart-subverting songs from American popular culture.

'I left my heart in San Francisco,' he trolled out to the backs of the houses.

He'd go back to the Zénob, talk to someone there, one night they'd let him sing and he'd be discovered. When he was a success, he'd give up playing the cello – which was what Simon thought he did – and take singing lessons.

Thus he proceeded through the spring night, under the hunch-backed moon of madness, past mundane garbage bins and the judgemental light of other people's kitchen windows. Through those windows he could see people talking, eating, and once or twice arguing. Passing a first-floor window he saw a young couple trying to calm a howling baby under the brilliant white glare of their kitchen fluorescents. He saw the look of empty despair that the young husband cast outwards to the black panes of the window.

Simon dimly remembered something like that in his own life. He must have had children somewhere. Perhaps his were in bed now. In all the other places the children were in bed. Or perhaps they were grown up. He wasn't quite sure, so he put his children out of his mind. Well, yes he was pretty sure they were grown up. And they were a part of his life that he mustn't think about. A current of cooler air blew some hairs from his beard into his mouth and he parted them with both hands.

Down a dark side passage between two houses, he caught sight of a man peeking in at a window until the man turned and saw him, and ran away.

'That poor idiot!' snickered Lucifer. *'What do you suppose he was up to?'* and went off into gasping snarls of laughter.

Simon and this man recognized each other. They both belonged to the community of driven souls who wandered the downtown slums and shrubberies at night. They never spoke to each other, but if Simon had already given some consideration to the life of this other outcast, it was because he felt superior to him. He pitied him. Trying to ignore Lucifer and his insinuating laughter, he sorted back through his recollections.

The peeping Tom, a pockmarked man with haunted eyes, had been a hairdresser in an earlier existence, and something had gone wrong with his life as well. Now he lived only at night and on the street. Sometimes in the summer he posted himself at the corner of the rue des Ursulines and Saint-François-Xavier, in a spot where young men leaned up against a three-hundred-year-old church and waited to be chosen by anonymous men in cars. The ex-hairdresser sometimes waited for a long time. He was too old for that trade. And now he was looking in windows.

So he's come to that, thought Simon, judging him from the security of his superior education, his music, his taste, his art and his schizophrenia. A word of Schiller's, from the line he had just fished up, floated to the surface of his mind. *Feuertrunken*, drunk with fire. It occurred to Simon, not for the first time, that the ravaged man might also be a pyromaniac and as a result he

64

was proud to have chased him off. He himself was after all a good citizen and immediately he could hear Lucifer congratulating him for having figured that out. But from somewhere deeper inside, from somewhere even the devils hadn't got at, he felt a kinship with the man and with his unexpressed sufferings. How events pour over our heads, he thought, and how we all slowly, inexorably descend, seeking some deeper level.

Simon had known a particularly bad period when he couldn't control his mind at all, when the chattering, accusing voices and the sudden visions of ugliness and deformity had taken over completely. It was during that time that he had lost his last business. He had difficulty thinking about that debacle, or understanding exactly what had happened, because his marriage had vanished at the same time. Had he ever had a wife? Of course he had, but he refused to remember. And yes indeed, there had been children. But no, he couldn't think about it.

Simon had been to a university, he had studied philosophy and economics. Later he'd learned accountancy. At some distant time in the past he had sold life insurance, and after that real estate. In the real estate business, he'd gone into partnership with others. But before he was diagnosed and before he had resigned himself to the drugs, before he even suspected what was wrong with him, he'd signed all the forms ending his association with the real estate agents who had been his partners in his last enterprise. Had he given money away? Probably. Of course, he must have. The truth was that he didn't know.

What he'd wanted then, more than anything else, was to break with the life he was leading. He'd felt trapped in his mind not only by a welter of thoughts and images that he couldn't control, but also by the demands of a job that he wasn't doing anyway. He'd go out to show a house, meet a client, and forget all about it on the way. People were constantly angry with him. He was confused and lost. Exhausted, he had wanted to be free of complaints and accusations, and after signing the papers he was, more or less. At least he was free to hallucinate. His former medical plan provided a pittance and there was always welfare. In his destitution, in the lucid times, Simon recalled the Roman proverb that tells us it is a terrible thing to be rich in a very poor society – because the rich are constantly obliged to defend their property, he supposed – but a wonderful thing to be poor in a very rich society. Thus he was lucky, he supposed. He had enough to eat and nothing to defend, nothing to lose. Well, there was his cello, but only that. He knew himself to be dependent on the social welfare system of what was at least a moderately wealthy society and, when his mind was clear enough, he tried to believe that he could live well on what they gave him. He tried to believe that he was living for his music. The rest of the time he dreamed and sang and played his practice pieces and talked to his devils.

The first year of his illness he'd spent alone with his cello in a tiny apartment on the third floor above the old tavern, Le Monastère, on Radisson. There was a layer of office space between him and the drinkers below who were, anyway, anaesthetized by beer and their own music. No one was going to complain about the noise when he practised his scales and arpeggios, which he did, obsessively, for hours each night. He argued with his devils about his progress. He recorded himself and when he'd finished practising, he would listen to his own études. He played them back for the devils, wanting to convince them of his worth. He turned the sound up and up and lay back on his couch, soaking it in, the raw, laboured, groaning noises over and over again. I did that, he told them, that's my music. He was proud of it.

Simon's music was the first and surest sign of his madness. In speech and manner he was usually polite, and even when he wasn't really rational, he was rarely aggressive, except when he was hallucinating. Occasionally he ignored some aspect of reality because he thought it was just another delusion, and occasionally he was angry, but it was the cello, more than anything else, that gave him away. With perfect seriousness, he would play those scales and études for anyone who seemed willing to listen and when he did, the disconnected growls and grunts and groans of the big viol, the tormented inadvertent harmonics that he seriously heard as music, left his listener astonished, embarrassed and distressed. Simon did know better – most of the time – than to mention the devils, but he never understood that other people heard only chaos in his cello-playing. He really heard music. Unfortunately it was a music that no one else could recognize.

Other than that, there wasn't much left for him to do but wander the streets of the town, sometimes disoriented and sometimes drunk, shocking former acquaintances when they ran into him unexpectedly. Although he was not always incoherent and not necessarily very dirty, he was certainly ragged. People would cross the street to avoid meeting him. Simon Lesieur had gone crazy and soon everyone had heard about it. They were frightened by the long hair, the frayed clothing and the puffy look. To them he was profoundly disturbing because they saw in him what they imagined might one day happen to anyone under stress, as if schizophrenia were not an inherited disease. But this was not understood. Stories circulated about a variety of events that were supposed to have driven him out of his mind, although no one tried to ask him what had happened. There were those who supposed that he might die soon, and probably some of them hoped that he would. They could never have suspected that Simon, seeing the former hair-dresser peeking into people's windows at night, felt an equivalent pity.

And after that first year of wandering, there had come an interval of weary clarity when he'd finally heard what the hospital psychiatrist was saying. He'd accepted the fact of his illness. He'd more or less stopped drinking and had learned to keep taking the Cogentin as well, even if he'd had trouble getting used to it and still hated it. It was during that time of shaky optimism that he had moved in with Jacqueline. She was a youngish woman who had taken courses at the university in social work and then had never found a job. She had a teenaged son and daughter who were home less and less of the time, and she lived in a large flat giving onto this lane just above the rue Sainte-Geneviève. That was the place he'd passed in his stroll tonight. At the time when she met Simon, she was already divorced. Her husband had been married to someone else for a quite a long time and Jacqueline was wearing a miniskirted uniform and working as a waitress in a fried-chicken restaurant.

Simon arrived at the northwestern end of the lane, went around by the rue Sainte-Angèle, and found himself facing the rue Saint-Maurice, which was also the main road to the Cap-de-la-Madeleine. Cars were passing here and the noise troubled him. It was an intrusion from the busy world of people with places to go. He stared across the street at the Super Carnaval supermarket, closed for the night, and its enormous empty parking lot. Nowhere to hide.

'Turn around,' said Satan, and he did.

He turned and walked slowly back into the darkness of the lane, observing how many lights had gone out in the past hour. The breeze from the east, freshening, had brought a layer of cirrus clouds that were starting to cover the moon, the moon which was higher in the sky and looking pale and distant. But his accompanying devils were still with him, if quieter now. They were reasonable tonight. For the moment, only a thin, high-pitched ringing in his left ear told him that they were present, that and the occasional deep chuckle from Beelzebub. Simon hunched his shoulders and went on down the lane, back the way he'd come, towards Jacqueline's house.

For a while he had believed that she understood his

problems simply because she said she did. Apparently she had persuaded herself that she could live with a man who might well begin to hallucinate if ever he gave up taking his medicine. In fact she had fallen upon Simon with exclamations of relief, and had confided in him about her previous difficulties with men. He was, after all, a man with an education. A gentleman. He'd had a business of his own. How lucky she was, she had declared, to meet such a straight, respectable man, after all the fools. About the cello, she had said nothing, and little by little he had given up playing it.

Simon walked on down the lane and soon he found himself outside her dining-room window again, still seeing light through the closed curtains. He shivered. They'd had a winter of happiness in there before his devils had caught up with him. It was on an evening in March, more than a year ago, that he'd drunk a whole bottle of wine at supper and then had lost his mind. Now he came closer to the window and leaned against the sill. While sitting at the table just in there, just behind these same yellow curtains, he had been shocked to find sneering demons rising up out of the corners of the room, not his familiar devils but strange, unknown demons that he'd never seen before, mocking, japing at him. Behind Jacqueline's head, her plants hanging in the window had snarled and bristled in his direction, and he'd seen weird lights strung among their fronds, flashing coded messages of insult and menace. As the demon voices threatened him, Jacqueline's face had turned into the snout of a pig. So she was a danger as well. And, although he couldn't remember it, they told him later that he had attacked her.

After that had come the police, the fast trip to the psychiatric ward at the Hôpital Sainte-Marie, and the long slow process, in the middle of the night, of finding a psychiatrist to admit him, while inside his head the new demons yammered on, contending with his resident devils and with the disgusted policemen supervising him. Afterwards the people at the hospital had taken two weeks to straighten him out. The only problem was that when they let him go, with a new prescription, he had nowhere to live. When he went to collect his clothes, his books and his cello from Jacqueline's place, there was already another man installed in her apartment, a short, muscular man with a gold chain, false-looking teeth and frizzed hair of a strangely consistent pumpkin shade. This man had greeted Simon with cool friendliness, kept him standing at the door for a long time, and finally handed over one of his boxes of books. Then he'd closed the door in his face and Simon had walked away down the lane with the heavy box in his arms.

Thinking about that man, with his teeth and his chain, he put both hands on the window sill and tried hard to focus his eyes through the coarse texture of the curtains. His devils came with him, peeking over this shoulder.

'*You nitwit,*' they sneered, '*leave that slut alone!*'

Simon wavered. He drew back a little. It was hard to defy the devils but he wanted a glimpse of her, just to see what she looked like tonight. He put his face close to the pane again. There were nights when she left these curtains open. He often walked past here and sometimes he could see her leaning her elbows on the table across from her new man, could see the man gesticulating, explaining, taking charge. Passing by out here in the dark lane, he could pause, furtively, to watch them eating supper together at the same table where he had drunk that last bottle of wine. Once he'd even heard them arguing about him, the frizzy-haired man claiming that something that was missing must have been carried off by Simon, *ton fou*, he'd said to Jacqueline, your loony. And Jacqueline had yelled back and said that he might be loony but that at least he was a gentleman and not a thief and a pimp.

It sounded in fact as if the frizzy-haired man had swiped whatever it was himself, which Simon was pleased to learn.

He'd been proud of her for defending him. True, things had finished badly between them, but for a time she had made an effort to understand him. In a way, he pitied her as well.

After the man had pushed him out, he'd simply walked down the lane, passing tonight's leafy hiding place without noticing it, and on along des Commissaires to the lowest, poorest part of town, not far from the paper mill and right beside the sewage pumping station. It was there, in the shadow of a mountain of pulpwood, that he had seen a sign, A LOUER, in the window of a rotting house, so it was there that he had gone. The place was dark and smelly but it was cheap and he had five rooms all to himself, therefore it was home. After a few days he had found the courage to go back for the rest of his boxes and his cello. Then he shut himself in and waited for his proper devils to return. But as long as he remembered to go for his injections, which was most of the time, they stayed away. And his neighbours, night people, fringe people like himself, had no complaints about the noise from the cello. Nor did they pay any attention if he talked to himself in the street at night. They left him alone.

At that point he had decided to use his mind again, starting to read in the eighteenth century, with the Encyclopedists. They appealed to him because he saw in them the last generation of thinkers to believe that human knowledge could be organized and classified in its entirety, the last to try to capture it all and write it down rationally before it expanded out of control. For Simon there were too many things that swelled and shifted and changed, then escaped him. And a writer like Voltaire had the added appeal of having been on the Index, forbidden by the priests, although that was long ago. So Simon had read a little bit of his *Lettres philosophiques* before giving up. The more immediate problem was that he couldn't control his own mind. He couldn't concentrate. And as he turned the pages, Voltaire had seemed to him disorganized and impulsive too, not all that rational in fact, so he closed the book. He put it back on the shelf with the others. It wasn't exactly a renunciation, he was still planning to read it one day, but for the moment he found it easier to go back to the cello, or just to look out the window at the pile of pulpwood and at the clouds moving overhead.

He didn't mind living in a slum, he told anyone who would still exchange a few words with him, he was well settled in. He slept during the day and read, or tried to read, and made his music at night. It was a sort of sabbatical, he claimed, and in a few months or a year he'd be better. Never did he admit his problems in concentrating, never did he admit how lonely he was.

Once he had told his psychiatrist at the hospital how solitary his life was, but that particular psychiatrist had his own enemies in the medical establishment, and he wasn't there any more. His replacement was a cold, defensively businesslike man whose eyes were like a wall and whose face never moved. As a part of his examination, he routinely asked Simon a series of questions about what he heard and saw, while Simon, looking at him there behind the desk, saw only a brick wall. He tried to deal with the nurses instead. They were the ones who administered the antipsychotic drugs anyway, and he had learned to go to the clinic at times when the psychiatrist wasn't likely to be around.

There was no one else who could be expected to endure the confusion, the mood changes, the anger and the genuine blank spots. The fears. Simon was condemned to solitude, so he prowled and this was what it had brought him to. Looking in Jacqueline's window.

But then, standing out there in the rising wind, he heard voices again, surely real voices this time and not his devils, coming from the other side of the yellow curtains. He backed away from the window. There was an argument going on in

Jacqueline's dining room. Angry shouts could clearly be heard through the glass. Simon's devils closed in around him, zooming up out of nowhere to watch the fun. They joined their cries of rage and glee to the sounds coming from behind the curtains and the windowpane, and over their voices Simon had difficulty understanding what was going on in there. Nevertheless he was sure that he recognized Jacqueline's voice flaming up in shrill protest against a darker screen of masculine snarls and grunts.

The sounds were being transformed into visual images, bright jagged forms flashing on the darkness and thicker, heavier shapes looming and vanishing. He would have found it difficult to peer through the curtains' texture at any time, and now there was a great deal more to decode. He couldn't be sure which images were the pineapples and parrots printed on the cloth, which were the human forms moving around on the other side, and which were pictures furnished solely by his brain. Nor was the confusion purely visual. The angry voices of the couple fighting clashed with the insistent, nagging voices of his devils and further scrambled the limits of reality.

There was more. Simon also felt guilty. He'd been through this before and it had been his fault. He'd acted illegally. The shame of that had never left him. And certainly now there must be something that he ought to do, but what? He was afraid. Satan told him not to be a coward so he went back and leaned cautiously against the pane, putting his eye close enough to the texture of the cloth to see more through it. There was lots of light in the room on the other side and he did distinguish human forms gesticulating. He saw an arm raised, and someone moving fast across the room.

'Ow! Arrête!!'

That was Jacqueline's voice. Simon felt something like an electric shock. He froze. A lull in the shouting was followed by the sounds of objects being smashed, first dishes but soon after that the heavier impact of furniture being thrown against the walls. The noise was actually travelling from the front room towards the kitchen and the back door. Simon remembered the cool arrogance of the man with the crimped hair and the big muscles in his arms. He was dangerous. As he advanced now down the length of Jacqueline's apartment, apparently tossing aside everything he found in his path, Simon heard him as the force of some natural disaster. Like a tornado, rumbling and crashing, the frizzy-haired man was cutting a swath of destruction through Jacqueline's belongings. So what had he done to her?

Simon's mind gave him a picture of a black cloud with huge ivory teeth, then a gaping purple vortex wearing a glinting gold chain. He shrank away from the window while Lucifer scoffed at him. Simon was an idiot, a wimp and a weakling. But Simon was past caring what his devils thought. He was starting to hyperventilate. The insidious wind blew his hair into his eyes and he whirled around, panting, beating it back, his heart pumping hard. He was looking for somewhere to hide, and quickly.

By the time the kitchen door crashed back against the outside wall Simon had squeezed into a narrow space between two garages across the lane. He'd forgotten his stroll, his songs and even his devils, pressing himself flat between the weathered boards, breathing in wood rot and getting a splinter deep in his lip. He chewed at that, feeling nothing. There was a sticky ooze running down his chin and he should have known that it was blood because he could taste it, but there was no pain. He hardly noticed it. What mattered was that the tightness of the space around him provided a sort of reassurance. At least that was a real perception. It provided some reference to the solid physical world. He pressed tight against the boards, gasping, gulping in the old-garage smell of dust and oil together with his own blood. He heard his devils shrieking at him to *do* something.

But there was nothing he could do. After the crashing inside the house came the sirens in the distance, and all of that was mixed up with the yells and exhortations of Lucifer and Beelzebub and Satan. They were laughing at the same time. They loved the whole disaster. And somewhere there was a dog barking – did Jacqueline have a dog? – and there were bells ringing too, big ones, like the cathedral bells, until at last, swelling above all the rest of the racket, Simon heard a symphony orchestra. Beethoven was back. He even heard the words about the holy sanctum again, but this time sung by a whole chorus:

> *Wir betreten, Feuertrunken,*
> *Himmlische, dein Heiligtum …*

And the evil, angry frizzy-haired man with the big arms was swept from his mind. The noise of the approaching sirens was far more than he could stand and he was in a panic of guilt, sure that he must have done something terrible, although he couldn't find it in his mind, whatever it was. For a moment he could see Jacqueline's face, screaming, then turning into something else, an ape or a dog, with fur around its eyes. He was terrified that he must have hit her again, and that was what had transformed her into an animal face. This had all happened before. And it had been his fault, it was all because he had failed to control his mind.

Simon cowered in the space between the garages. He cried out to Beelzebub that it wasn't supposed to happen again. He'd been treated, he had promised (*had* he promised?) to go regularly for his injections. Could he have forgotten to do that? He no longer knew. But whatever was occurring, whatever had been done, of course he was going to be caught and blamed. They were going to come and grab him and twist his arms again, and hold his head so tightly that he could hardly breathe, then push him into that back seat the way they had the last time. Panic-stricken, Simon wept while Satan, Lucifer and Beelzebub sat on his head and roared with laughter.

While all these things were raging in his brain, from his hiding place he had a sudden view of a monstrous gargoyle with writhing snakes for hair and a twisted, fanged snout. This was the frizzy-haired man, moving with what anyone would have seen as a strange, stiff-legged gait, who had just crashed the back door open. Spouting *tabarnaques* and *câlisses*, the man flung himself down off the porch and into his car. Jerkily, raging like some devil incarnate himself, he slammed the rusty machine sloppily into reverse and accelerated away with a sidewinding lurch that should have taken the tires off the rims. Even through the approaching sirens, Simon and Satan and the others could hear the car squealing off into the distance, skidding round the corners of the mean streets down by the paper factory, then farther off into the night, still audible blocks away.

Trembling, sweating, drooling blood, Simon pressed his face into the boards of the garage. He didn't know what to do. He didn't know whether he was aggressor, saviour, or a simple survivor. Should he knock on the door? Should he rush in there and ask her for forgiveness? Or should he run down the hill to his own house and close and lock the door and get into bed? Should he telephone her? But he wasn't supposed to. They'd told him that. There was nothing Simon dared to do. He just hoped that she was alive. He had no certainty at all of what he himself might have done or not done but he thought that he did see her shadow run past the curtain inside. However, he couldn't move, there were lights going on and off in his brain, and the devils wouldn't let him think. When all he wanted was to do the right thing.

When the pitch of Satan's howls and Lucifer's screams began to blend in a strange dual register, the lights in his brain blazed up so brightly that they hurt him. He screamed with the pain and was further confused by his own voice. He couldn't grasp that what he was hearing were the police sirens arriving in the lane. When they stopped suddenly, the silence was almost like losing consciousness. But revolving red reflections were probing his hiding place, slashing blades of light stabbing for him. His heart blanked and thudded and then, just as suddenly, the flashing lights went out. Everything was black instead. He couldn't see.

Simon had realized, he had only just realized that it was the police. This was it. Here they were. Jacqueline had called them. That was an experience which he remembered clearly in spite of himself, being grabbed and twisted and held down so expertly, the smell of the men and of their uniforms, the sharp scratchy texture of the upholstery in the back seat of the police car, and its vomit smell, and all the bright lights afterwards. His devils were still screaming at him to stand his ground but he couldn't. He slithered from between the garages and rushed gasping down the hill. Simon forgot where he lived or that he lived anywhere. Instinctively, he ran back towards the dark stub of the lane with the swarm of devils flying at his shoulder. By this time they'd changed their minds too.

'Run,' they howled, 'run!'

And he did. He'd had enough of sirens, enough of police and hospitals and authorities.

'Hide in the leaves, get your ass in there!' Satan shouted, while Beelzebub barked noises of disgust and contempt and Lucifer made another visual appearance, suddenly capering along ahead of him, sniggering and making obscene gestures.

Simon plunged into the dark space under the leaves and crouched in the hollow left by the dead Volkswagen. He wrapped his arms around his head, covering his ears against the sirens even though they had stopped. The police wouldn't find him here. Nobody could find him here except his devils. They whooped and yowled. They shrieked contradictory orders at him but Simon didn't move. He stayed where he was.

The police didn't find him, but only because they weren't looking for him – and because they'd had all their lights trained on the house when he slipped out behind their backs. For fifteen or twenty minutes more, he heard a hubbub of activity up by Jacqueline's house – cars slamming on the brakes, doors opening and closing, different voices jabbering together. Unless it was more demons. Simon wasn't able to go and look. The sounds ended. He crouched lower, then lay face down on the ground. There was nothing he could do. Even after the police cars had gone and quiet had returned, he remained there, motionless, hearing less and less human activity anywhere, then nothing, then only the wind blowing through the leaves. Although he believed that his devils had remained with him and were watching over him, they kept their mouths shut.

The night was still densely black when Beelzebub suddenly prodded him.

'Sing.'

Reminded of his vocation, Simon rolled over. He unwrapped his arms from his head. Cautiously, he peered up through the leaves and branches. He shifted his cramped legs and sat up. It was cold now and his lacerated lip, black with dried, stiffened blood, was swelling. But he noticed none of that. He took a deep breath.

'Come on, sing!' said the hectoring voices, 'let's hear you belt it out!'

Simon put both hands on the ground and shifted, with difficulty, to a crouching position. Slowly, awkwardly, he stood up. He opened his mouth and panted for a moment, looking out at the street and the sleeping houses, at the untrodden gleam on the sidewalk. The night was not quite black after all. It was greying just a little and he didn't like it. But he bit at his lip and stretched out his jaw. Then in the late-late early morning, his voice, hoarse and frightened but still in tune, quavered up out of the leafy darkness beneath the cement wall. He was doing his best to please his devils. Still more of Schiller's words filtered through from his memory. They seemed to offer comfort.

> *Deine Zauber binden wieder,*
> *Was die Mode streng geteilt;*
> *Alle Menschen werden Brüder . . .*

The words of the poet told him that happiness, that enchanted state, would bring into the fold all those who were customarily, forcibly, set apart and excluded. The last line said that all men would be brothers. There was more after that, in fact there were further verses that he couldn't remember at all, but Simon didn't care because now he heard a whole orchestra accompanying him, the swell and rush of the strings and the poignancy of the woodwinds against a solid background of brasses. He saw the hallucinatory sounds transformed into colours, although he could not have said what colours. It was a light show. It was sheer beauty. The enchantment picked him up and whirled him along like a chip on a wave. *Freude.* Joy. Creation of the gods.

Unable to feel pain or cold, Simon did feel an overwhelming effusion of bliss. Singing, he believed that his devils were his defenders. He believed that they had saved him from danger and that he was singing to please them. He also felt a wave of generosity. Surely everyone had a right to some form of happiness, however personal and peculiar, and among other things he wanted Jacqueline to be happy, and to forgive him. For what? He tried to remember. Perhaps it was the other way around. He decided that it was he who should forgive her. Jacqueline should be free too, she should be free to live any way she chose. If she wanted to cohabit with a frizzy-haired demon wearing tombstone dentures and a chain of golden barbs, well, just because that was her pleasure, he wished her joy. To each his devil.

But being hauled off to the hospital by the police was not a part of any state of contentment. This time he could rejoice because they hadn't got him, whatever it was that he might have done. And he wasn't alone because his own proper devils were there with him, listening. He started his song over again:

'*Freude, schöner Götterfunken . . .*'

The leaves over his head shifted and flurried in the rising wind. The weather had changed overnight. It was very cold. And the pulpmill stench was stronger, a sharply sulphurous, burnt-cabbage-soup smell. He didn't mind any of it. Feeling strong and brave, Simon stood up among the saplings and pushed them aside so that he could reach up through them towards the racing clouds. He wanted to celebrate life. Stretching out his arms, he projected his voice and sang in a loud, clear, carrying tone.

'*Tochter aus Elysium . . .!*'

Somewhere above him and behind the embankment, a watchdog came rattling out to the end of his chain and began to bark. Somewhere else a window clacked open. And not long after that, in the pre-dawn gloom, lights were going on in the downhill house. None of it meant anything to Simon, but this time his singing had not gone unheard. It was producing a response.

The branches around him rustled and gushed and turned over as a spatter of rain fell through them, bringing down bits of leaves and their gluey husks, which caught and stuck in his hair and beard. With the east wind announcing the dawn of a grey and sleety day, Simon stood singing in the trees. Wearing only a polyester shirt and his torn jean jacket, he was blue with cold. His straggling hair was stuck with bits of the trees, his face and the hands he held up to the heavens were black with the oil that had long ago leaked out of the old Volkswagen, and his mouth was bleeding, but he went on singing about joy and brotherhood. He didn't even realize that his faithless devils had fallen silent. With the coming of cold daylight, they'd all ridden off on the blustery wind, leaving Simon to other authorities.

The Best Time of the Night

From the rue Sainte-Angèle, from the warm summer night, Jacques could probably be seen through the screen door as he bent over the sink, washing dishes by the little light installed under the cupboards. It was nearly two in the morning but this was the best time of the short, precious summer night and since he couldn't bear to go to bed, there were possibly others out there who felt the same way, walking or cycling through the soft supportive air. They might well look in here and see him. But that didn't matter to him and he didn't lift his eyes from his work. He wasn't expecting anyone, he just wanted the door open. He was enjoying the contact with the summer air.

Behind him the cat sat on the kitchen table, keeping him company, staring raptly out into the darkness. Although she seemed pleased that her human companion was still up to share this moment of the night with her, she was also interested in what might be happening outside. Every now and then an insect knocked at the screen and her eyes dilated. He had offered her food, but she wasn't hungry.

Tomorrow was Saturday – in fact it was Saturday already – and Jacques was washing his week's dishes. He'd come home from work, made and eaten his supper, taken a shower, and then had fallen asleep in front of the television news. When he woke up it was after eleven o'clock and he felt refreshed and alert. But for what? So he had read for a couple of hours and now he stood in the low light of the quiet kitchen, wearing an old striped bathrobe, methodically washing the dishes. He used a dish mop for this operation and all his gestures were gentle and precise. He mopped each object inside and out, then rinsed it individually with very hot water from the tap. With the wrung-out mop, he wiped up every drop that fell and he set each plate and cup in a predetermined order in the draining rack. From time to time he heard the cat behind him growl at something on the other side of the screen but he paid no attention. It had nothing to do with him, it was only some feline danger, some other cat probably.

He could also hear the paper mill rumbling away at its night's work only three streets east of him but that didn't bother him either. The dull grinding noise was a sort of accompaniment. And the mill was modernized now. There was rarely any odour, although people in Trois-Rivières claimed that the smell of the paper mill was a harbinger of rain. He wasn't so sure that was the real order of things. When the paper mill managers decided to release whatever part of the process it was that caused the stink, they seemed to choose a day of high wind or rain to do it. Not that it happened that often any more. There appeared to be some awareness of public opinion now.

But the paper mill smell was one of the many reasons that his wife had given for leaving. She had also said that she had to get out of this little town, especially out of this poor section of the little town, and away from the smell and the unsuccessful people, into the city. As if there were no poor people in Montréal. For a moment Jacques leaned into the sink, resting his weight on his hands in the warm water in the bottom of the dish pan. There was nothing left to wash. He looked around the kitchen for forgotten coffee cups.

It was true, there was such a thing as a smell of poverty, but it was difficult to analyse exactly what it was. It came from the spaces people lived in. Decades of rancid cooking grease perhaps, combined with old tobacco smoke, mildewed cloth, sweaty human bodies, decaying food, rotting wood. And yes, some of his neighbours carried this sharp, special smell in their clothing, as did some of the students in his classes. No matter how clean and bright they were in themselves, it clung and it gave them away. They came from the poor district. He sniffed in the air in the kitchen, coming in from the summer night. It smelled sweet and fresh to him. But he had lived here for so long that he, like the others, might not realize it if his old house stank and imparted its essence to him as well. But not this house, no, surely not, he thought as he wiped the counter, because it had never been rented out, it had always belonged to just their family, had always been kept clean.

In fact this was really Céline's house. It was she who had inherited it. When they were married she had given him half of it, and now she had left. The other half, her half, hung over him, unsettled. He couldn't afford to buy it.

It had never been entirely clear to him whether Céline was abandoning him or whether she was simply leaving Trois-Rivières. They had both been in their forties, their daughters had moved out, and now Jacques was nearly fifty. At forty-three Céline had gone back to work. She'd had a job as a secretary for a real estate office. But then she'd taken a course, become a real estate agent, and soon after that the little city with its tightly interconnected society was too small for her. Everyone knew everyone else. Everyone knew whose secretary she had been, whose wife she was, who her father had been. For some reason that had bothered her, when it was simply the truth. That was the way it was supposed to be, he told her. This was her home town. Of course everyone knew her. But she had decided that she was stifling here. The time had come for her to move to Montréal. And although he had never tried to stop her, he had never understood either.

It seemed to him that at his time of life a man should have nothing to prove, that he should be able to take his woman for granted, to find her in his bed at night without having to argue and reason and persuade. That was all he wanted. He wasn't interested in other women. Glamour had no effect on him. He was a monogamous man and all he wanted was his own wife, whom he had married more than twenty years before, with the firm intention of living out his life with her. Surely this was every decent man's right. Why had this happened to him? He was sure that he had done nothing to deserve this solitude.

Now that the dishes were stacked in the draining rack, he turned to the rest of kitchen. He disturbed the cat to wipe the table top and then he wiped down the surfaces of the stove. The cat followed him, rubbing against his ankles. His bare feet stuck a little to the floor in front of the stove. The floor always seemed to get sticky there, but he had to walk around barefoot to discover it. He would wash it, maybe tomorrow. He was a stocky, heavy man, and the old wooden floor under the linoleum sagged a little as he padded from the sink to the table to the stove.

The house had been built by Céline's grandfather before the turn of the century and soon it would be a hundred years old, a settling frame structure enclosed by the working-class tenement houses of the nineteen-twenties and thirties. Most of them were three stories high, built in attached rows with the long twisting outside staircases that gave each of the six *logements* in a building its own balcony and its own front door on the street. But Céline's grandfather had been a builder and a man of substance. Jacques's house stood alone, with a double door in the middle of its gingerbread front porch, and a side porch running along to the kitchen door, which was now open to the night. It looked welcoming.

This was the kind of house where families of ten and twelve children were supposed to have been born and raised, but this one had never housed a sprawling gaggle of offspring because Céline's family had not been prolific. She was an only child. And Jacques himself had been an orphan, adopted from the *crèche* by an ageing couple who had died when he was just out of his teens. When Céline had complained that everyone knew who her family was, he had envied her for that. He wished he knew who his parents had been. And since he couldn't supply himself with a family in the past, he wished that they could at least have had more children. But somehow that hadn't happened. He and Céline had just two daughters, girls who had both left Trois-Rivières as soon as they finished Cégep.

And after they were gone, Céline had been more and more restless, almost as if she were jealous of her own children. She was dissatisfied with the neighbourhood her family had always known, this little grid of four or five streets spreading east from the town's centre and down towards the St Maurice River and the paper mills. She saw it as poor and backward and constricting. But to Jacques, who did not know if his ancestors had lived here or anywhere else, it was home, and it was a source of comfort and interest. It was a village. He observed the comings and goings around him, the students, the old ladies who knew everyone and everything, the regulars at the *dépanneur*, the neighbourhood eccentrics, and the madman who wandered all summer long wearing the same shirt, disturbing no one as he conversed, intimately, with his hallucinations. Well, perhaps there were some who would have locked him up, but Jacques was not among them. Once, late at night, Jacques had seen the man with a polystyrene cup in his hand, playing in the fountain in the Ursuline sisters' garden. Crouched on the edge of the basin, he was catching the running stream from under the spout, then pouring it carefully back into the pool. It was obvious that he was working intently and methodically at producing something both useful and necessary for his lonely private world.

Jacques found that there was nothing left to do in the kitchen, so he poured himself a glass of orange juice and stood at the door considering the façades of the houses across the street. In the summer the town was never fully asleep. There were still lights on over there. Through the curtains of one upstairs window he could see the changing flicker of a television set. As he gazed through the screen, a police car cruised past with a soft whisk of rubber on warm asphalt. They went by here regularly every night. That was something else he had learned since Céline had left and since he had taken to staying up all night, studying the darkness, the obverse of the normal daylight world.

Trois-Rivières had once had the reputation of being a tough town but that was no longer really true. That was a hangover from the old days of the log drive and the fur traders and the Indians from Odanak, the days when there was only a ferry to the south shore, before the Pont Laviolette was built. Now the logs were hauled by trucks, the fur trade was supposed to be immoral, and the Indians, discouraged no doubt, but understanding Europeans better than before, stayed home and watched television like everyone else. Now even the police department had been cleaned up. And the mill workers had moved away from these densely populated streets and gone to the suburbs, where they could have little vinyl houses with lawns and above-ground swimming pools. The long family *logements* housed mostly students and retired people these days. The only warring elements, the ones whose presence had truly humiliated Céline, were the welfare families, and they were very limited in their territory, generation after generation being born, fighting and dying within the same four streets. Those who were born north of the rue Sainte-Geneviève stayed there, and those who were born south of it had mostly declined into incest and alcoholism and died out. And anyway, they had rights. They had been rooted here for centuries. People forgot that the town was nearly four hundred years old. Layers of human hope and despair had accumulated here.

Even his house, itself only about ninety-five years old, was strangely square because it was built on massive stone foundations that probably dated from the French régime. This might even be the third house to have been built on them. And he didn't care if he was south of Sainte-Geneviève, in the oldest, shabbiest part. He didn't care if the dynamic element of the population always moved onward and outward, if even the mill workers now thought this neighbourhood beneath them. He was on solid foundations and it was quiet here. This house, and Céline, were the only roots he had ever known.

Yet it was Céline who had been unable to accept his contentment here. He lacked ambition, she said, and she had tried hard to push him beyond what he was doing, which was teaching in the secondary school. During the seventies she had seen others move on into the Cégep system, then into the provincial civil service, *la fonction publique*. Many of them had expense accounts now, and went on business trips to Europe and Asia, while he continued teaching the same basic science courses, reading books that amused him, watching television. He supposed that Céline might have felt cheated precisely because his pleasures were simple. She must have expected more from him. After all, he was intelligent. During their twenties when they, their society and everyone around them had been in a state of dazzling expansion, he must have looked as likely as anyone else in their group of friends to make a splash of some sort. But she had invested twenty years in him only to find, at the end of that time, that he was contented, satisfied with his quiet life and happy with her. Why should she have been so disgusted by that? Why shouldn't a woman be pleased that her husband was content?

He found he was still standing in the kitchen door. He looked down into his empty glass and decided to have another, this time with some vodka in it. The liquor cabinet was in the living room and in there he was confronted with his daughters' graduation portraits. He gazed into their smooth, confident young faces as he reached in among the bottles. They were as ambitious as their mother. One of them was in Montréal at the moment, working at some kind of public relations job, and the other one was in Europe. He wondered what it would have been like to have a grandchild, to assume the mantle of the grandfather. But neither of his daughters was married. He supposed that they must have boyfriends, but he didn't know. Back in the kitchen, he poured orange juice in on top of the vodka, stirred it, and went out to sit on the front porch.

Now was the truly peaceful, private time of the night, getting on towards three in the morning, when the town belonged only to a few nocturnal souls who passed in the street without looking up at the porch or speaking to him. The cat came with him and jumped into his lap. All the lights across the street were out now, except for the television watcher. Jacques didn't know who lived in those rooms this year, but it must be someone as solitary as himself. The aluminium chair squeaked beneath him as he settled back to watch the moon travelling across the sky.

What was wrong with the women anyway? What had got into them all? Why did they all have to have cars, gold earrings, and two dozen pairs of shoes? He saw the full range of variations on this theme not only on television, but also amongst his colleagues and in the streets and the stores and the daily life around him. They all had to have careers. They were usually alone. But sometimes he would see them in restaurants on Friday or Saturday evenings, in groups of five or six, ordering wine and flashing their credit cards. If they had small children they had left them with husbands or babysitters. If they had grown children they were competing with them. They took care of no one but themselves. That wasn't the way it was supposed to be. He didn't understand. He had nothing to say to any of them, and no interest in whatever they might say to him.

Surely it was normal and right that a man who was nearly fifty should have his woman by his side? After all the years they'd spent getting along together, it should be so simple. How could he look for another woman? And why should he have to? Anyway, none of them would be interested in him. He shifted his weight in the flimsy chair and drank, stroking the cat. A few weeks after Céline's departure, one of her co-workers from the real estate office had called him up and had talked at him until he understood that he was being encouraged to ask her out for dinner. Too surprised to do anything but comply, he had, once.

She had been very direct with him. He literally couldn't believe his ears. After supper and over the Grand Marnier she had told him that she was willing to be his *amie*, his girlfriend, if he would get himself a better car, if he would have a proper suit made, and if he would quit smoking.

Well, he had stopped smoking – and just the thought reminded him of how much he missed it – but after that single date he had never called the woman back. It hadn't been diffi-cult to end the flirtation because it seemed she had a strict accounting system for her friendships. As she had explained it to him, since she had called him, the next time it would be up to him to call her. That was how a relationship worked, she had said, *kif-kif.*

'I called you this time but now it's up to you to call me, to show you're interested.'

So he simply hadn't called her.

Delicately, one claw at a time, he unhooked the cat from his bathrobe and lowered her to the floor of the porch. She drifted to the end of it and disappeared into the hedge while he stood up and went inside to get himself another drink. In front of the refrigerator he remembered that his elder daughter had tried to give him advice about women. She had explained that, since women were no longer economically dependent, a man now had to think about being attractive, seductive even, just as women always had.

'Before, women had to put up with everything,' she had

said, 'bad breath, dirty feet, infidelity, violence, because that was the only way they could eat. Men made an effort while they were courting and after that they didn't bother because they didn't have to. The woman was caught ...'

Jacques closed the fridge and came back out onto the veranda. Caught. Had Céline felt trapped with him? He watched the cat slinking across the empty street, going somewhere on cat business. He had been insulted by his daughter's remarks. As far as he knew, he did not have bad breath. And he was clean. He was faithful, he was civilized. It seemed to him that she could use some advice herself, on how to catch a man.

'Now a man has to be seductive too,' she had said, 'and he has to think about keeping a woman's interest, because she doesn't have to stay with him for any material reason ...'

There might have been more than that to her argument but he hadn't followed it. He'd stopped listening. Material reasons. While she talked, he had remembered paying for her education and for having her teeth straightened, her imperfect bite being a legacy of one or other of his own unknown biological parents. He sat down again, heavily, in the flimsy chair and set his glass on the porch beside him. He remembered rushing her to the hospital when she was three years old and had a high fever and convulsions. He remembered the night that he and Céline had spent waiting there. He had thought that these were deep commitments, that he was attached, that some things were inalterable. But no, he was supposed to be seductive. He took a deep breath. That remark had really shocked him, especially from a daughter to her father. For a moment he actually ground his teeth. Then he looked for the moon, but it was out of sight.

Somewhere to the northwest, probably in the rue Saint-Maurice, he heard a police siren start. It came closer, wailing through between the houses, and died away a couple of streets over. Must be in the rue Hertel, he thought. There was still some of that. Violence. There always would be. Céline had been right, in a way. He called this a quiet neighbourhood and it was, but there were still fights and men still beat women and sometimes killed them. That could happen anywhere though. And it did. In fact it was probably worse in the suburbs where it was done in privacy. Here, everyone knew. Was it worse now because a man was supposed to be seductive, he wondered? Could his daughter have laid out her very rational arguments about economic independence for some of these guys who weighed two hundred and fifty pounds and could drink a whole case of beer? After all, everyone always had been equal when on welfare. But no, he put the thought from him. His daughter, for all her education, maybe because of it, was an innocent. He clenched and unclenched his fists, which were as large and hard as those of any of the working or non-working men in the streets around him. All sorts of things were possible, but he was a peaceful man.

Then he listened through the darkness. Now there might be the slamming of a door, shouting, screams and curses. But there was nothing. Only the cat reappeared from across the street with her tail all puffed up. She threaded swiftly through the shrubbery and leapt, weightless, to the porch, while looking behind her as if she'd seen a ghost.

In public, at work, Jacques studied the women around him all the time, trying to understand what had happened. They were all ageless now, all younger than he was, their small, brightly painted faces almost invariably flanked by large, flashy earrings. That had been a shock too, when Céline had come home one day with hardware in her ears. It wasn't right. Her plain, unpunctured ears had been fine when he married her. There was something barbaric about pierced ears, and something that went against all their rhetoric of liberation, or so it seemed to him. One should accept one's body as it was. But sitting there in the dark with no one to see him, he ran his hand over his own head, which was getting balder week by week. He'd had a full head of hair all through his thirties. Why did it have to happen now? They said it didn't matter, but it did.

Maybe he would call Céline in the morning. She often called him on weekends and recounted her week's activities. At least they kept in touch. And he and she had never quarrelled about domestic things. He was the better cook but she had always kept the house clean and done the shopping. For such a long time he had thought that they were perfectly happy. They had married for life, when they were both very young and their hormones had been predominant. Sex had solved all problems then. And he had assumed that there would never be anyone else, that there would never need to be anyone else. He still wondered what Céline had assumed, if anything. That he would become some big businessman in town? That he would build her a spreading modern bungalow on the St Lawrence and take her to Chamber of Commerce dinners? Or should he have become an assistant deputy minister and bought her a house in Québec City? He just didn't know. One of these days he was going to have to talk to her, to really try to find out what she was thinking.

There had been no drama, no obvious rupture, to her departure. First there had been just the secretarial job, then the course in Montréal, then another, then some sort of convention. The real estate job, when she had started, had been supposed to be in Trois-Rivières. But the market here was small and cyclical, and soon after that it had been two days a week in Montréal, then a week, then two weeks, until there came a time when Céline would actually call him to tell him that this week she was going to be home for the weekend. She confessed to him that she had nothing to do in Trois-Rivières and everything to do in Montréal.

For the first time in his life, he had felt the sickness of jealousy.

'Who is he?' he'd wanted to know.

But no, she said, it wasn't that, it was her job. To his amazement, she had even invited him to come and live with her in Montréal, because now she was making more money than he was. So he believed her when she said that there was no lover, but somehow that made it even worse. And how could she say that she had nothing to do here, when he was her husband and he was here? Besides, he hated the big city more than anything else. And there was really nothing for him to do there.

The cat, her tail deflated, jumped onto his knees again. As he stroked her, he looked for the television glow in the window opposite, but even that had gone out. A police car turned the corner from the south and spurted past him, silently, with someone in the back seat. So that was settled, whatever it was.

Then he saw that the dark sky was just beginning to be ever so slightly paler than it had been. From somewhere a bird produced one clear annunciatory note, which was followed by a sleepy chirrup from somewhere else. The night was gone already and he had nothing figured out. But maybe now that Céline had been in Montréal for a while, now that she'd had a chance to get Trois-Rivières out of her system, she'd be able to tell him what it was she wanted from him, apart from her objections to this town and this neighbourhood. He decided that he'd call her in the morning. After all, hadn't she been the one who had made the last telephone call? *Kif-kif,* he told himself, my turn to call, to show that I'm still interested.

Then, not wanting to find himself out on the porch in daylight, he pulled his bathrobe around him, picked up his glass and the cat and went inside. He closed and locked the kitchen door and turned out the counter light. In the bedroom, the cat jumped onto the bed, purring. It hadn't been his idea to acquire this animal, it was Céline who had wanted a cat. But now he had a cat. He pushed her firmly to the foot of the bed, where she stretched herself out, purring loudly, working her claws in the folds of the turned-back bedcovers and gazing into his eyes with tolerant feline assurance. Before he got under the sheets Jacques closed the window against the birdsong, then drew the blind carefully down, to keep out as much light as possible.

Gambler's Fallacy

A mutter of thunder crossed the sky and Pierre, from the window over the kitchen sink, looked out towards the north end of the field. He was just in time to see a thin violet snake split the grey above the woodlot. The first hurricane of the season was working its way up the American coast from the Gulf of Mexico. The barometric pressure was dropping, and although there was a feeling of apprehension in the air, in Québec there was no rain, only this dry lightning, when it was rain they needed. They'd been waiting for it since the snow melted, the parched weeks stretching out one after another and the new vegetation thrusting up out of the remaining moisture from the thaw and run-off only. Under its surface greenery, the earth was nothing but dust.

The flash in the sky gave Pierre a queasy feeling along his palate and the back of his throat. He needed a drink. He needed more than a drink. Papers rustled on the table behind him as his mother turned them over. Without looking, he knew the smoothness of her hard-worked fingertips on the documents. From overhead came the hum of the fluorescent lights and, turning from the window, he took in as never before the thick gleam of the walls and cupboards, painted year after year.

His father's house was his house now. It wasn't poor but it was humble. The smell of stored cabbages and potatoes filtered up from the root cellar under the kitchen floorboards, the rank odour of rural conservatism, generations of it, prudence and thrift for tomorrow and next week and next year, the never-ending digestive process of living. For Pierre that smell and the long view of the fields from the kitchen window called up long-buried memories of adolescent despair and nihilism, of wanting badly to get out of this place. He had escaped from it for a while, for most of his adult life in fact. For years he had turned his back on this, his parents' world, where people waited for the rain.

The lightning, the ominous charge in the air, made the tension more troubling. All small perceptions – the smell, the reflections of light on painted surfaces, the auditory volume of the room – were amplified, and with them, other awarenesses. The reality of death and the futility of life expanded to fill the space between Pierre and his mother.

Looking past her and through the archway into the dining room, he could see the television set, which was on but with the sound turned down. Across the screen there paraded images of people in Florida as they lined up to buy canned food and bottled water. This was their hurricane ceremony, an annual event. The Americans took it for granted that they were in the centre of the action. A man hammering plywood sheets over his windows smiled and shrugged. He was used to hurricanes. Pierre envied him his danger. Whoever he was, he'd identified the problem, knew what it was, where it was coming from and what to do about it. Pierre looked down again at his mother and over her shoulder at the papers. His father's will had left more money than either of them could have imagined. *'Tu devrais voir l'Europe,'* he told her, *'et Paris ...'*

Images of Europe, of France the motherland, and above all of the fabled city of Paris rose up in the kitchen between the son and his mother. For both of them it remained a mythical place. Of course they knew people who had been to the French capital, had walked its streets, eaten its food, and complained about its prices. But that made no difference. Paris remained a place beyond the real, loved and feared with an ancestral reverence.

Sadly, Pierre's mother looked up from the table. She was strong and big-boned, almost as tall as he was, and a habitually silent woman. Since her husband's death she had suffered not only by the absence of her life's partner, but also from the necessity of facing the world and speaking, even to her troublesome son. Her broad hands covered the papers from the notary as she studied his face, while Pierre, looking down into her eyes, clearly saw that his mother really did not want to go to Europe. In the quiet kitchen, she cleared her throat before she spoke. *'C'est toi qui devrais y aller,'* she said. It's you who should go. And although she did not say so, he realized, as he should have earlier, that his mother would not have had the faintest idea what to do with herself in a country where she had no family. He shouldn't even have suggested it.

Then she added that anyway the money wasn't just for her. A tremor crept into her voice as she spoke. Her husband's will, his bank accounts and his life insurance, had provided an income for his widow, more than he'd had when he was alive and certainly more than she had ever seen. Now it was difficult for her to know what attitude to take with the son who had been such a disappointment to his father.

And when Pierre saw her puzzlement, her amazement even at her new position, a stirring of guilt was added to the faint nausea in his throat. She must be wondering how to cope with her newfound power, wondering if in fact she could tell him anything.

She did try. *'Avec Andrea ...'* she said. *'Tu devrais y aller avec Andrea.'* That he should visit Paris with Andrea. She was offering to pay for a trip to Europe for the pair of them.

During these past months, Pierre had been careful not to mention his ex-girlfriend. For most of his time with Andrea, ten years and more, his mother had distrusted her and it was only a couple of years back that she'd made the effort to welcome her. That was on a quiet summer evening when Andrea had been invited out to the farm, had met his parents and had sat making careful conversation over supper in the dining room. Afterwards they'd drunk coffee on the back porch while they watched the swallows dipping and plunging between the trees. Andrea had gazed out over the sunset fields and had glanced across at Pierre. His father and mother had liked his girlfriend after all but their acceptance had made it difficult for him to smile openly at her, or even respond to the look she threw him. And now that she was a part of the past, and his father was gone, his mother held out this enormous concession. It came to Pierre that she had never had the chance to be generous before. She was trying to please him. He found that he couldn't answer her and he turned back to his view of the long field and the grey sky.

After all, the money *had* been left entirely to his mother. It was only the house and the farm that he was inheriting. That was his land out there now, those were his furrows reaching back up into the hills, two miles and more, with bush beyond. Already they were green with weeds. As for the house, the handsome traditional timber house with its curving eaves and broad porches, for years painted and propped and hammered back together by his father, it was still his mother's home and it loomed as a responsibility. It was a good house, he knew that, there was no rot beneath the paint, but all the walls and woodwork were clotted with some sixty seasons of cream-coloured enamel. No cupboard door closed properly any longer, the windows stuck and the kitchen floorboards were humped and scaled with dark green paint. There were too many layers to be removed and too many layers to be added to. Pierre straightened his back and took in a lungful of the farm-kitchen smell. He was as little equipped to deal with agriculture or general maintenance as was his mother with airlines and hotels. Nor had he been ready for his father's death. The long weeks of his dying had served only to drive Pierre's anxieties deeper into his secret soul.

Needing a cigarette, he made a circuit past his mother at the table and out onto the side porch. His father had died of lung cancer and it upset her to see her son smoking. He also needed to get away from the silences, the intermittent rustle of paper and the melancholy vegetable stink. He looked down at the porch floorboards, battleship grey here, but just as thickly painted, and took another deep breath, hoping to feel better in the open air, although the temperature outside was exactly what it had been inside the house, the atmosphere still and the sky a dense, meaningless white.

'Just keep her company for a few days,' the curé had said. 'Don't leave her alone with her thoughts.'

Dealing with the village curé had been the strangest part of his return to his parents' home. Pierre Arcand was forty-seven and had spent the best part of his life writing songs. He'd made his living playing piano and guitar and singing in the smaller clubs, at first in Trois-Rivières, more recently in and around Sherbrooke and Montréal. When the call had come about his father's illness, he'd been in Montréal, trying to put the small-town scene behind him. And because his parents, this farm and their village, fifteen miles out of Trois-Rivières, came from so much further back even than that, he felt as if he'd been lifted into some earlier incarnation. When had he ever had anything to do with a priest? This one, a public-relations type, not much over thirty, had been suavely businesslike. He must have sized up Pierre's long grey hair and had also taken note, possibly, of the drug-light glowing in his eyes, then had treated him tact-fully. There was no pastoral role to be assumed, so their exchanges had been simple: the details of the funeral service and the burial, the fee for the local gravedigger, the contribu-tion to the church. The undertaker and the hearse were paid for separately. The cemetery plot was there already, populated with aunts and grandparents and his only brother, dead in infancy years before Pierre was born. But plenty of space was left for the remaining family – for Pierre's father and mother and Pierre himself and any children that he might have. Therefore the priest's recommendations about his mother, which could have been seen as comforting, instead struck him as frighteningly pragmatic. Just keep her calm until her time comes, he seemed to be saying, because there'll be room enough for everyone.

Pierre's paper-sorting sessions at the kitchen table had been different from hers. Instead of cheques and certificates, he'd had an ambulance bill for his father's trip to the hospital in Trois-Rivières and a bill for the private room there. There was something about income tax remaining to be paid, and there were questions about his father's last pension cheque, as well as a notice about two late payments on the tractor. The hydra-headed bureaucracy of death, quiet enough while his father was still legally alive, now gaped and reached for him with its many mouths.

From the porch, his eyes roved to the shed. He hadn't known about the new tractor but it must be in there. It could be sold, no doubt, or taken back to the dealer. As for his father's car, it was the elderly, well-maintained Chevette parked beside the peonies just here at his feet. He stared through the railings at it. That he could use. In fact he had been using it for weeks. It was paid for. He shifted his gaze to the flowers, into their disorderly pinkness, swollen and dishevelled. Peonies usually bloomed just as the first summer storm arrived to break and scatter them. This time the storm seemed to have stalled and the frowsy petals hung there, turning brown.

The sense of mortality around him, the smell of the peonies decomposing, the colourless sky and the falling barometric pressure, the dead man's car and the locked tractor shed all made the world pressing in upon him appear newly finite, so that his own failures, his age and lack of accomplishments rose up before him, followed by the image of Andrea. In his mind, she wasn't really gone. Oh yes, she had let him know that she was through with him. He knew that. It was just that he couldn't feel it. At some other level, some other sector of awareness, there was an understanding that remained to be settled.

Pierre knew that what he needed now was to go into Trois-Rivières and look for her. She must still be in the apartment, because their lease wouldn't have expired yet. He could try to talk to her. Or he could make the rounds, find other friends. After all, he did have friends in Trois-Rivières, even if Andrea didn't want to see him, because that was where he'd started, in the Café Zénob. That was his other inheritance, besides this farm, this village and all his ancestors buried here, going right back to the beginnings of New France. In Trois-Rivières, the Zénob was where he'd made his start as a poet and a musician, and it was there that he had first met Andrea, a tall girl whose sherry-coloured eyes exactly met and matched his own.

He supposed that she would approve of his father's having been buried from the church in an old-fashioned village funeral. She'd be pleased, surely, at the way Pierre had assumed responsibility. He wished she could have seen how politely he'd handled the curé, how respectful the man had been. Maybe she'd changed her mind by now and was ready to take him back. He dropped his cigarette to the grey-painted boards and flattened it with his sandal, knowing well what his father would have said at seeing him scar the paint. A small thing, but he could do it now if he wanted to. He pushed the butt over the edge behind the peonies and lit another. Then he walked to the railings at the end of the porch and stared back at his land.

Pierre's field was a long narrow Québec farm, measured in *arpents* rather than acres. That was for the length. The papers in the kitchen said that the width was measured in chains. Chains. He imagined his ancestors and their neighbours stretching a heavy chain across the furrows, laying it out and picking it up. This much is mine, yours begins there. Then walking on up the field to measure it again. Dragging their chains. He looked farther. The wooded ridge at the far end had some maples but they were grown in and sheltering a lot of other trees. At some point his father had stopped cutting firewood. Pierre had noticed that the house had electric baseboard heaters but had no idea when they'd been installed. The woodstove was gone and the house, built with boards and timbers from the same bush, had ceased to consume its descendants. Pierre remembered the making of maple syrup from his childhood, so he knew that there must be a sugar cabin back there in the woodlot – if it was still standing – and beyond that two or three more miles of woods, he wasn't sure how much. All that would be in the papers under his mother's hands on the table.

They said that the house at his back had been built by his grandfather in the nineteen-twenties. The land across the road, which fronted on the St Lawrence River, had been sold for cottages in the nineteen-fifties. That was when it was still possible to swim in the river. Now the cottages were gone and there were three big vinyl-clad houses across the road, each one worth more than the original farmhouse, all of them blocking access to the water. But the money from the sale of that river frontage had provided at least a part of Pierre's *collège classique* education.

He'd been sent to the Séminaire Saint-Joseph in Trois-Rivières, where fate had made him part of the very last generation to do classical studies. For him, secondary school had meant Latin and Greek, rhetoric and versification, history and mathematics, plus the great nineteenth-century French poets and dramatists. But in the year following his graduation, the Cégep system had taken over, with courses in sociolinguistics and psychology and the history of religions. The literatures of Greece and Rome and France were all forgotten together, to the new bureaucracy all equally ancient. The result was that Pierre and the others from his year were left stranded on a cultural promontory overlooking nothing.

At the time, he hadn't cared, he hadn't given it a thought. He'd gone with the current of the times, had scraped through the last of his courses at the Séminaire before chucking it all and taking a job as a cook on a lake freighter. That had been new and strange, plying the Seaway up to the Lakehead and back through Toronto and Montréal, sometimes as far as Québec City, living with men who knew nothing of his family or his village, and who also seemed to have some very wrong ideas of what French Canada was. Although he'd learned a sort of English from them and was able, just barely, to laugh at their jokes, he had soon realized that he could never explain his true world to them. The first time he had seen Trois-Rivières from a ship had helped to put the problem into perspective. After leaving Montréal and passing Sorel, they had steamed down through Lac Saint-Pierre. They'd sailed under the big new bridge. And then for a few minutes, Pierre had stood at the rail looking hard at his home town, so small behind its piles of pulpwood and its cathedral. But that was all that the men on the ships could ever know of it. When they passed the village a little later, he'd barely glimpsed the church over the treetops. Then they'd rounded the headland and Pierre's childhood and adolescence were gone. Before dark they were in Québec City, tied up behind a cruise ship, hearing self-assured, cynical New York voices: 'Wheah's the *sordy-exit*...?'

In the off season he'd written poems, played the guitar and then, beginning to be known in the small world of the arts, had quit the boats and moved back to town to make a meagre living in the various bars and clubs. In Trois-Rivières he was known as a *chansonnier*, and it was possible that the priest who had been so noncommittal with him had heard of him. Less generally known was the fact that he'd been in Montréal since the winter, living on welfare, writing some of the time and trying all of the time not to give in completely to beer and drugs. It was his mid-life crisis, or something like it, prompted by the breakup with Andrea, then interrupted by the call to come and sit at his father's deathbed.

Andrea. How he wished his mother hadn't said anything. He wasn't going to go to Paris, either with or without Andrea. That much he had in common with his mother, although some of his reasons were different. Pierre had heard of the air pollution and the roaring traffic as well as the astounding price of a cup of coffee, but it was more than that. He was unwilling to discover what the modern French city had become, unwilling to find large parts of his dream cancelled by reality. He'd been working hard, too, at putting Andrea out of his mind. Yet he kept returning to the problem of needing to tell her what he was going through. He glanced in through the kitchen door and saw that his mother was gone from the table. The accumulation of papers remained. She must be upstairs, sorting his father's clothes. Pierre mashed the butt of his third cigarette, observed only by a robin sitting on a wire, then stepped down off the veranda and started up the tractor path beside the field, turning his back on the closed doors of the machine shed.

It was just possible that his new status as a landed gentleman might bring Andrea back. It was six months since they'd split. She'd kicked him out at New Year's, when he'd got blind drunk. In fact Pierre had been blind drunk almost every weekend during his last year with her but he didn't consider that. He remembered only that last terrible evening, and he remembered only the beginning of it. That was New Year's, however, that was the frozen season, whereas this was June, even if it was a stagnant grey spring. In theory at least this was the season for new growth, and rebirth with the spring rains, if they ever came. Still feeling the need for more air in his lungs, Pierre lengthened his stride and kept walking. He could at least walk back and take a look at his property.

Halfway up the field, the land began to rise in a way he hadn't noticed from the kitchen window. A shallow depression crossed it here, once an irrigation ditch probably, now filled with berry bushes. He paused and looked back over the furrows, then down at the earth. Scraps and stubble remained from last year's corn harvest but were rapidly being swallowed by other growth. Weeds grew whether it rained or not. Nothing had been planted, but unexpected hollows were blooming with daisies and buttercups. Seen at close range, the field was not a featureless stretch. Small animals had left the traces of their daily excursions. There were groundhogs' holes and birds' nests in the rowan trees along the path. And the earth itself was a slightly different colour up here, and sandier looking. Everywhere the land had conformation, individuality and meaning. The greyness and immobility seen from the house were no immobility at all. Birds and insects were busy all around him.

Pierre knew that it was his father, still working, still planning for the future, who had turned this field under last fall. He knew that when eventually he went to inspect the tractor, he was going to find it properly oiled and ready to be fuelled up and driven out. He was sure though that the time for seeding was past. When the date had come to put the crop in, his father had already been in the hospital. Which meant that his father's death had been the death of the crop for the coming year. Under the heavy sky, and without having made any decision to do so, Pierre kept walking. He tramped on up towards the trees, wondering about the cabin and wanting to see if it was still there.

When first called back from Montréal, he had come only as far as Trois-Rivières, not to his parents' house. For a month or more he'd stayed in a room above the Zénob. From there he'd gone to the hospital every day. Evenings he'd spent down in the bar, drinking coffee or de-alcoholized beer, always hoping to see Andrea, who never showed up. Yet he had continued to expect her. He was sure that she must know, she must share the atmosphere of calamity that oppressed him at seeing his father gasping for breath and slowly, hideously, inflating. He wanted her to know about the determined effort he was making not to get drunk. What he was hoping for was a reward. And some-times, in the Zénob, he talked to the girl with the blue eyes instead. Unfortunately she had been a part of his break-up with Andrea, although she was only twenty-one and hadn't taken him seriously.

It was late at night in those weeks that he would go out and walk past the apartment on Sainte-Cécile, never seeing a light in any window. If Andrea was up there, she was asleep. Then he might try to feel jealous, imagining her with a new lover in her bed, although he didn't believe it. He was sure that she was alone and he hoped that she regretted him, hoped that she was secretly waiting. But his father's long dying had invested all of life with a sort of paralysis, so that he'd never done more than stand on the street, looking up at the windows. When he went back to the Zénob after that, the girl with blue eyes would be gone as well. It was at such times that, once or twice, before going to bed, he'd allowed himself a real beer.

As his father's condition worsened, he'd moved out to the farm and chauffeured his mother back and forth to the hospi-tal. Only once, on the road, had she ventured to ask him about Andrea and he hadn't answered her that time either.

Pierre and Andrea had lived together for nearly ten years before she'd started to become difficult. The problem seemed to be that, unlike Pierre, she had become aware of the passage of time. She was thirty, then thirty-one, then thirty-two, a good fifteen years younger than he was, but she'd decided that she wanted something stable. Painting the kitchen cupboards in the flat on Sainte-Cécile, she'd announced that this was the very last time that she was going to paint a place that didn't belong to her. She'd talked about children and for a while she'd made fusses over other people's babies. All that had seemed normal enough to Pierre and he'd ignored it, but then she had started going to mass. She would go to the cathedral in the afternoons when he was just getting up and rolling himself a joint. Suddenly everyone connected with religion, the people he'd always laughed at – and she had always laughed with him before – were automatically *good*. '*Qu'elle est bonne!*' Andrea had said of a hardworking intellectual nun well known in town for her energetic commitment to helping alcoholics and rehabilitating drug addicts.

And Pierre was astounded. He was suspicious. Soeur Surprenant might well be admired for being tough, perky and good at handling the media, but the thought that she might be seen as *saintly* – which was what Andrea meant – was bizarre. What on earth had got into her? She'd quit smoking, then she refused to touch alcohol. She even stopped talking about having children. In fact she talked less and less, and sometimes he had caught a look of condescension on her face when she came home in the afternoon to find him still in bed.

Pierre left the track and crossed into the ploughed field, where he picked up a chunk of earth. He had no idea how to farm the land. Some of the neighbours were probably watching him out here right now, laughing at him, the only son who'd gone to the city. Naturally some of them would also be making plans about how to get his land away from him, cheap. There were two or three Belgian families in the village now and they were always eager to buy farms that were not being worked. One of them had already been to see his mother when he wasn't there. He closed his fingers on the clod in his hand, finding that even under the clouded sky it was warm from the sun's radiation. Maybe he should have tried to tell his mother about Andrea. Maybe explaining what had happened, making their split official, would have forced him to accept the situation himself. But he couldn't, he wouldn't. He would never have left Andrea for the blue-eyed girl, although there was more to it than that.

He crumbled the chunk of soil in his hand. It was powdery dry, although the weeds all around him were flourishing. There was a roll of thunder and, as he let the dusty earth sift through his fingers, he saw another jag of sterile lightning crack the clouds above the trees. This year, for the first time in his life, Pierre had taken the time to observe the change of season and to understand that the dry spring was a real problem. Day after day, the clouds hung there, dispensing nothing. Therefore it didn't matter if no crop had been put in, because it was going to be a bad year anyway.

Of course he'd always known that the farm would come to him, but not so soon. His father had been strong, hardworking, organized, and had certainly not expected to die in his sixties. Nicotine was an insidious thing. Pierre wiped the grains of earth from his hand on the seam of his trousers and pulled out a cigarette, looking up towards the trees, then back down towards the river. At this point the rise in the land became more obvious. From here he found that he was actually looking down at the house and the road. And suddenly he was struck by the unusual emptiness of the scene. There was no traffic. Birds were calling to each other and a bee or two zoomed past, but today there was no human activity, nobody in the other fields, no sounds of machines working, nothing, not even the Belgians with their big Belarus tractors. The warm earth spread itself to the white sky and occasionally the sky rumbled back or stabbed at it with a flash of heat lightning, but there was

nothing more. Weeds grew, but not perceptibly. At the far end
of the furrows, between the clouds and the road, his house
crouched in its carapace of paint, its metal roof glinting dully in
the humidity. It looked small.

The house had significance though, because it stood on the
north shore of the St Lawrence River. This was the king's road.
Highway 138 or *l'ancienne deux*, old Highway 2, was the one-
time *chemin du roi*. The highway had been called that since the
seventeenth century, even if no king of France had ever set foot
or wheel upon it. Pierre knew that in the nineteen-sixties
Charles de Gaulle had made a point of using this road, rather
than the south shore autoroute, for his ceremonial progress
from Québec City to Montréal. The locals claimed that the old
general had noticed the façade of the village gas station and
had remarked that it was the first time in his life he'd seen red-
painted *fleurs-de-lys*. Pierre could just make out the flat roof of
that gas station between the green masses of the trees. Across
the neighbours' fields was a clearer view to the village centre
and the twin spires of the church. He could see movement
there. A procession of some sort was bumping through the back
street that ran from the side of the church and out to the cross-
road to Saint-Luc-de-Vincennes. A couple of wagons pulled by
tractors were carrying a flutter of blue-and-white flags, small
distant figures waving them. *'Vive le Québec!'* The cry came
faintly across the weedy land. And again, *'Vive le Québec!'*

Then Pierre realized what the date was. This must be the
twenty-fourth of June, always called *la Saint-Jean*, even if the
holiday was no longer a religious occasion. Now it was the Fête
Nationale. That would be why the fields were empty. He
watched as the parade went round again, down to the highway,
past the church and back out to the Saint-Luc road. There
seemed to be no one else watching it. Maybe they were celebrat-
ing inside. He turned and tramped on over the furrows towards
the woods. His sandals, gritty inside, raised little puffs of dust,

while the light from the sky overhead, diffusing blankly through the grumbling cloud mass, was devoid of any clear angle and offered no shadows. It was impossible to tell what time it was. The air remained neither warm nor cold but simply present. Pierre paused to take off his sandals and shake them out.

He was as much of a nationalist as anyone else – the bullying ignorance of the men on the boats had taught him the need for that – but he could also remember a time when the festival of St John the Baptist had been a genuinely religious occasion on the village calendar. And it did seem to him that there should be more to that procession, maybe not the yellow-fringed silken banners and gilded statues of the old days, but something more celebratory. Once, as a small child, he'd seen a wagon covered with flowers and drawn by someone's prize bull. *La Saint-Jean* had included blessings and bonfires and large outdoor family gatherings. There were magical things as well. Surely there'd been a belief that if you washed your face in a running stream early on the twenty-fourth of June – or was it just before midnight on the twenty-third? – it would cure something, he wasn't sure what. Not cancer or alcoholism, certainly. But he hadn't had a drink for more than a week, not since the morning when the hospital had called and told his mother to come quickly.

At the upper end of the field, before he could get to the woodlot, Pierre had to push through a prickly mass of wild raspberry bushes. They scratched his arms and tore at the sleeves of his shirt. Then he found himself at the edge of a real irrigation ditch, waterless now but seven or eight feet deep and filled with shoulder-high ferns and a thick spread of poison ivy growing up its banks. He stood over it. There was no other way through to the cabin, even supposing it was still there. He hadn't thought to wear boots. He looked across into the canopy of the sugar bush. From the treetops, the birds were screeching warnings to each other. They battered in the leaves and whistled their possession, not wanting this intruder in the lower level of their domain, while Pierre, hearing them, staring into the trees and back down at the shiny leaves of the poison ivy, was already thinking of something else. He was remembering that John the Baptist, in the religious procession, had always been played by a little blond boy with a white lamb in his arms. A picture of innocence. The wall of vegetation across the ditch from him was a densely woven interlacing of trees, bushes and vines with no obvious opening anywhere. Where was the way in? The track must be overgrown. There were fallen trees in there too. It was a jungle with no trace of any pathway.

Swatting at the wave of mosquitoes that had arisen from the coverts and come out to eat him, Pierre retreated to the field. Later in his life, John the Baptist had been a solitary prophet living in the desert on locusts and wild honey. By that time he would have been a wild man, brown, bearded and fanatical. He had starved and had visions, but all the while, inside, he had also been that little boy with the lamb. Pierre struggled with this idea, with its implications. There was more to the story. Out among the furrows, thin and square-shouldered, bearded and wild-looking himself, Pierre considered the value of deserts and dryness and sunlight. He'd never seen a desert but he was sure that there must be a clarity there, an absolute cleanliness. At least a desert would never grow into a monstrous, biting green tangle like his sugar bush. What a colossal task his father had assumed in trying to control and cultivate the land. The work. That was his inheritance, just work. Hard labour. Chains. As for the cabin in there, Pierre decided that it must have been swallowed up long ago.

He started back towards the tractor path, under the massed clouds. Where was the American hurricane now? Was it still on its way? There was no change in the atmospheric oppression and he continued to feel slightly sick.

Then, while he was out in the open, if not all that far from the row of scrubby trees along the side of the field, an intensely white-violet flash suddenly split open the space around him, cancelling and absorbing all sensations and perceptions. The air itself seemed to have been sucked away. And the blinding light was followed immediately by a huge rolling explosion. The violence of the crash and the wave of ozone that spread out after it felt and smelled like intentional malevolence. There was a moment of mauve in which Pierre actually tasted the electrical charge in the air and realized his danger for the first time.

Standing out here, he might quite possibly be struck by lightning. There were statistics about this, so many farmers in so many fields killed by lightning every year. Somewhere he had also learned that he had a better chance of being struck by a lightning bolt than of winning the lottery. A moment ago lightning had just missed him.

Which was more dangerous, he suddenly needed to know, being close to the trees or being the only vertical mass out in the field? To his astonishment, Pierre found that he was shaking. He wet his lips, swallowed and ran his hands up and down his arms, experiencing the tremor of an unfamiliar emotion, something he had not felt for at least the past year and maybe longer. It took him a second or two to identify the feeling. It was pure joy. He was amazingly glad to be alive. And he was already a winner because the impersonal malevolence had spared him for something else, something more out of life.

By the time he reached the tractor path, he was beginning to revise his notions of statistics. The lightning had barely missed him. Obviously, therefore, his mathematical chances of winning something else must have been increased. It might be a sign. On the universe's colossal wheel, his ball would have the chance to drop into some other pocket. His life could come together. There was still time. Andrea would forgive him. They could live here, have children, and carry on the tradition his ancestors had left him.

Well, he conceded to himself that there might have to be some modifications. The barn could be converted to a sound stage. Some neighbouring farmer, maybe one of the Belgians, might be interested in renting the land for hay or corn. Or he and Andrea could grow organic vegetables on part of it and stock the woodlot with deer or wild turkeys, while he was recording compact discs. After all, why not? Fate must have spared him for a reason.

As for the hurricane and the Americans, who seemed to take it all as part of their cultural glamour, a chance to occupy centre stage, smile for the cameras and generally display their courage and resourcefulness, what were they really doing? Nothing much. Just running from a big wind. Pierre longed to see palm trees bent down flat to the earth, stretching out their fronds under sluicing floods of rain. I'd take my chances with the wind, Pierre thought, go through the eye of the storm, run the risk, whatever. Standing out here could be the test. What was luck but fate? What was fate but luck? And the land needed water. Maybe he should do a rain dance. He stepped away from the hedge again, off the tractor path, and tramped back out into the weedy furrows. Kill me, he said to the clouds overhead, and they ignored him.

Pierre was usually surprised when he didn't win the lottery. There at least, he reasoned, his chances were as good as anyone else's. Life was unjust but fate was arbitrary and required no skill or special knowledge. So whatever was wrong with him, with the choices he had made and the turns his life had taken, should make no difference. The vanishing corridor of years could be redeemed. Forgiveness for his mistakes was out of his hands but it was not impossible. As long as he was alive, the mechanisms of time and chance could do their work. It was true that since his father's death, time no longer appeared as open-ended as it once had, but it was still there in front of him. And destiny, whatever that was. Of course Andrea was right to want children. Then he remembered the time she had tried to persuade him not to buy lottery tickets.

'You have ONE chance in fourteen million,' she'd told him, 'you can't even begin to understand what that means.'

'No,' he said, 'but I've got two numbers. That means that I have one chance in seven million ...'

Andrea had thrown up her hands.

Now Pierre looked back towards the village for the procession, but it had stopped somewhere, or passed out of sight. He didn't really care. They always said that you couldn't win if you didn't gamble and Pierre wanted to gamble.

The winter before, as Pierre had slipped into a brown fog of marijuana and beer, Andrea had become ever more devout. At Christmas she'd gone to midnight mass but had merely looked distant when he'd offered to go with her. Since she hadn't encouraged him, he'd stayed home. Then on December thirty-first, in the afternoon, she announced that she was going to spend New Year's Eve with her parents instead of going to the Zénob with him. *'Bon, d'accord,'* he said, angry but unable to find any other answer.

And went out alone that evening and got really helplessly drunk, reducing himself to mindlessness, falling on people, kissing other men. *'C'est juste physique ...'* said one of his friends, jovially. Just physical. No emotional involvement, no commitment – haw, haw – then hit him, if not very hard.

On New Year's Day he'd woken up in his own bed, his and Andrea's, but with the blue-eyed girl beside him. That was a bad mistake, he knew. Even if the girl did leave before Andrea came home, it was clear that things were really finished this time. Pierre had gone back to sleep, alone, and when he woke found Andrea standing over him. In a clear, level voice, she gave him an ultimatum: either he gathered up his things and left, or she would. So Pierre arose shakily from bed, took some books and some shirts, his parka and his guitar, his bank card and his bank book with eighty-four dollars in it and went to Montréal. That was the last time he had seen her.

But now, with a house and a field, maybe he could offer her what she wanted. And yes, they could be married, here in the village, by that conveniently uncritical priest. That should suit her, and they could live in his ancestral mansion. Unfortunately there was still the question of money, even if the lightning had missed him. He didn't have any, and he couldn't put his mother out of her home either. Something would have to be negotiated, but it could be done. He looked up at the sky and down at the earth and walked on a few steps over the thirsty furrows. This land was intended to produce food, such a subtle process and so hard to believe in. Food out of dust. He scuffed his sandal in it, feeling his palate and the back of his throat stretched and dry. He was thirsty. A day or two of rain would transform this field. Another crack of lightning from farther off above the trees was followed by a very strange sensation.

All at once distinct currents of air were buffeting back and forth around him, gusts of warmth followed by the writhing passage of something cool.

Pierre looked up towards the woods. What was it, where was it coming from? He wasn't imagining it. He shuddered as soft heat brushed his hands and face and was gone. There was no wind, yet a body of tangible coolness breathed against him and dodged aside. Invisible movement was all around him. Tingling with the expectation of more lightning, he was seized with an even weirder impression. It was as if he had suddenly found himself in the midst of a battle, or the reverberations of a battle that had taken place here, right here in his field, but centuries or millennia before. It was surging all around him, not as a vision or anything he could hear, but like a tactile recall of long-gone conflict. Unseen forces were clashing and struggling, kicking up the air currents. Who were they, what were they? Transfixed, fascinated, Pierre felt his hair shift slightly on his scalp. This field had belonged to his family right back, great-grandfather and great-great-grandfather. They'd been here for almost four centuries. Had anyone ever said anything about an armed conflict? With whom, the Indians, the English, the American revolutionaries? Pierre had never heard it mentioned. Or was he capturing the echo of something even older? Humans had lived here for what, twenty thousand years?

Now he was sure that lightning would strike him and he waited for it. Instead there were more gusts of impact, bodies meeting and falling, soundless and invisible, but densely present all around him. Heat and coolness. And still nothing to be seen or heard – but then again – yes, dry lightning and distant thunder, like a gigantic music whose rhythms were too drawn out for him to grasp. It growled away downriver while Pierre stood marvelling at the contact with invisible warriors and weapons, advances and retreats roiling through the air.

Forgetting all about the neighbours who might be watching him, he walked backwards and forwards trying to find the thick of it, sometimes losing and then recapturing the currents of battle. Increasingly, he lost them completely. Still he walked in circles trying to seize the sensations as they receded. Finally they were gone, reabsorbed into the ether. Yet he was convinced that he had felt something real and that it had spared him, Pierre, when it could have destroyed him.

That was when it came to him at last that danger, risk, was in itself a form of absolution, whether he'd won or lost. The blind gamble of standing out in the thunder, under the expressionless sky, and of giving himself up to the electricity of the air offered a way of moving back through the countless layers of lost chances and therefore through all of lost time and vanished history, because he was still alive and survival was paramount. The merest moment could redeem everything. He breathed deeply, his heart pounding. Turning in tighter and tighter circles, eventually he came to a halt, staring at his own feet.

It wasn't simply because his mother had mentioned Andrea. He was still thinking about her every day anyway, about the way she'd waited last winter, with her fingertips on the kitchen table, for him to finish gathering his possessions and leave the apartment, her complete silence since then, and her darkened windows. After the years they'd spent together, so much remained to be settled. And despite his detachment and his exaltation, that momentary sense of electrified immortality, Pierre was filled with human longing. If he was going to be granted another chance at anything, then it should be another chance with Andrea. On the way back down the field, he would have liked to fight someone or something, if only he'd known what, but there was nothing to fight, no clear opposition, not even the wind. And the way back seemed longer. Tramping the dusty track, he fixed his gaze on the end of the field, at his house huddled between the road and the river, compressed between the land and the enormous sky. Now it seemed like a relatively unimportant part of his inheritance.

Quietly, he mounted the porch steps and opened the kitchen door. The documents from the notary were still on the table but his mother was not in sight. Over the papers, Pierre hesitated, feeling interest for the first time. He knew how old the house was but they might tell him how long the land had actually been in the family, if there had ever been any disagreements about who owned the upper field. He heard his mother's footsteps from the room overhead and went into the dining room. The muted television was still on in there. The Americans had reached the stage of putting hampers, bedding, lawn chairs and electrical appliances into the trunks of cars. As he moved through the archway from the kitchen, his mother appeared on the stairs. She was on her way down from the bedrooms with something in her hands, but when she saw him she stopped halfway, her mouth pinched with grief, and Pierre quickly looked away. He kept his eyes on the television screen instead, where a woman with a long-haired dog in her arms was waving to the camera. Whatever his mother was holding in her hands was something she was going to try to give him. He noticed the dog was wearing a barrette between its ears.

Then his mother spoke his name and he had to face her. He looked up. She was holding out a pair of shoes, shiny and bent to the form of his father's feet. His father's Sunday shoes. In one movement, Pierre backed out of the archway and took the car keys from the hook beside the back door.

I'm going into town, he said, and he left her on the stairs. He was out the door before she could speak, catching only the start of something she was trying to say about supper. He pushed the door firmly shut behind him, forcing the latch against the paint. He wasn't hungry.

Pierre had been driving the car for weeks but it was only in these last few days, since his father's death, that he'd been troubled by the act of sliding in behind the wheel. Now with his hands on the steering wheel and his feet on the pedals, he was newly aware of being enveloped in his father's smell and held in the shape of his father's body. Fitting into the hollow worn in the seat by a man who was lying in his grave was like fitting into his inherited destiny, in this case a destiny that he, Pierre, had not chosen, one which he had in fact rejected years ago. Could he get used to it? And where was he going and what did he think he was doing? There had to be more to destiny than this. He jerked the little machine into reverse and backed it out onto the highway without checking the rear-view mirror for trucks. As he turned west towards Trois-Rivières a robin, probably the same robin, hopped up from one branch to the next in the silver birch tree by the corner of the house. It trilled its twilight song into the stillness after him.

But Pierre, in the timeless grey afternoon, had forgotten that even on the twenty-fourth of June night would come. It was only as he slowed in the rue Sainte-Cécile that he noticed the time on the clock in the dashboard. It was past nine. And there were no parking places. The centre of the little city was swarming with people and cars, and he decided not to go to the Zénob straight away. The best thing would be to park in the unused spot behind Andrea's apartment, so he put the Chevette there, using the space for the first time. He got out of the car and looked up at her windows. He took as long as possible closing and locking the car door, and putting the keys in his pocket. He checked the other pocket for his cigarettes, then decided not to smoke. Behind him was the lane, in front of him the spiral stair up to the back door of the apartment. The windows were closed. There was no movement at the door, but ... well, nothing ventured, nothing gained. Pierre bounded up the rickety steps and knocked, then rattled the kitchen door. Nothing. He no longer had the key. Leaning over the fuel tank, he tried to peer in past a bamboo curtain that he himself had tacked up. Inside was only darkness. Andrea wasn't home.

However, the lane below him and the street at the end of it were filled with shapes and the scuffle of feet, groups of people heading down towards the port. Some of them carried folding chairs and drinks coolers, some led or carried small children. The Americans on television had been preparing for a hurricane by heading for higher ground but the citizens of Trois-Rivières, loaded with picnic supplies, were thronging the other way, down towards the river. For the second time that day, Pierre had to think for a moment to realize what this was about. Of course. They were hoping there would be fireworks for *la Saint-Jean*. Last year – or was it the year before – there'd been a fireworks display over the waters of the St Lawrence and the best place to see it had been from the Terrasse Turcotte. Pierre tried the door behind him one more time, then gave up. He went back down the steps and joined the crowd.

Suddenly it was real night. The sky was still clouded but the disappearance of the light had worked its summer magic. Some of the air's oppressiveness dissipated, while the blackness overhead seemed deeper and the temperate darkness, enlivened by voices and peopled with the soft multiplicity of many footsteps, took on a festival feeling. Pierre went with the footsteps out into the rue Sainte-Geneviève.

And it was through that pliant sound, the passage of many human feet, that everyone heard a yielding metallic *whonk,* the unmistakable sound of one car hitting another, after which the footsteps became a patter of running. Instantly there were more people in the street, a barefoot rush over cement and asphalt as whole families poured out from porches and balconies. Mothers ran in housecoats and slippers, holding the hands of little children in pyjamas, all eager to see.

At the corner of Sainte-Ursule a small car, failing to stop, had knocked another small car into the street sign at the rear of the armouries. The first car had bounced off and crashed into a porch, where it sat wearing the splinters of the steps across its hood and windshield. The car against the pole was beginning to smoke as three people got out of it and joined the circle watching. They seemed curiously uninvolved as a flame appeared out of the engine. Small and thin, the tongue of blue fire ran lightly and intelligently to the back of the car, where it caused a muffled thump. *'Aaahhh ...'* said the watchers as the burning gas tank set fire to the back seat.

From the rear of the crowd, Pierre saw a passing taxi driver speaking into his radio. More people were arriving at a run and, as the crowd retreated from the heat, the circle enlarged and there was room for everyone to enjoy the blaze. Someone told someone else that there were children trapped in the back seat.

The owners of the car said nothing. A strange calm prevailed as the car burned and the street sign on the pole above it twisted in the mounting heat. Then a fire truck arrived and a fireman, calm and businesslike, used a small axe to tap holes in the windows of the car. He poured foam in and white smoke billowed out and settled in the still air. It turned out that there were no children in the back seat. As the flames vanished, a faint air of disappointment set in and people began to wander off. The mothers with babies led them back to their beds. Pierre heard one of them saying to a friend, *'Viens t'en, on va manquer la loto.'* She didn't want to miss the lottery results on television.

At the same time, looking through the thinning smoke to the far side of the crowd, Pierre realized that he was looking at Andrea. He'd been seeing her for perhaps as much as a minute without recognizing her. And she was staring back at him, ironically it seemed, as he stepped across behind the last accident-watchers. She had changed in some way. *'Bonsoir, Pierre ...'* She smiled at him as from a height of lofty wisdom. *'Ça va bien, toi?'* From her tone, she might have been speaking to a casual acquaintance, maybe even to a child, certainly not to anyone of importance to her. It wasn't just irony in her voice, it was something colder.

Then Pierre saw her better. She was thin, extremely thin, and was dressed in a plain, heavy dress that seemed not to have much body inside it except for a pair of hunched shoulders. Her pale feet were bare and virtuously flat in heavy brown sandals. *'Andrea, je te cherchais ...'* Which was true, he had been looking for her, but not for this. As he kissed her, he felt her shoulders bony under his fingers. There was a fringe of moustache on her upper lip. She'd never had hair on her lip. Her breath was bad too, rancid-smelling. Something had happened to Andrea. Her eyes were the strangest of all. Even under the dim illumination of the streetlights, they were dilated, with a yellow gleam at their centres. Yet she returned his stare with perfect passivity. *'T'es ben maigre,'* he said. You're so thin. *'J'ai fait une retraite,'* was her answer. A retreat.

Andrea was pursuing her spiritual quest. Immediately he understood. She'd been fasting. What he smelled on her breath was the stale odour of sexless sanctity and an empty stomach. As for the look in her eyes, it was more than irony and more than pity. What he saw there was real contempt. She despised him for remaining unilluminated, while she had seen the truth.

Transfixed by those strange eyes, Pierre backed off a little. *'Je voudrais te parler, Andrea.'*

'Je n'ai pas le temps,' she said, *'je m'en vais chez une amie.'* She wasn't interested in talking, she had no time for him because she was on her way to see a friend. A female friend. Already she was turning her back with that arrogantly humble stoop and shuffling off into the dark. And irresistibly, the face of Soeur Surprenant rose in Pierre's memory. Would that intelligent woman really want to associate herself with this mad-looking scarecrow, dragging her pale feet in penitent sandals? Probably not. Amazed, confounded, he watched as Andrea hunched off up the street. Stooping smugly as if to shield some precious secret, she threaded her way through the last bystanders and vanished into the rue Saint-François-Xavier. Pierre closed his eyes and opened them again. Yes, she was gone. Andrea had neutered herself. The woman he'd known – or thought he had known – had ceased to exist.

With his back to the remains of the accident, the flashing lights of newly arrived police cars, a tow truck and some men attaching chains to the burnt-out hulk, Pierre forgot all about the fireworks at the port even as people continued to stream around and past him towards the river. Was this what destiny had reserved for him, was this all it came down to? He turned to walk back to where he'd parked, then hesitated and stopped. That was Andrea's place. He stood on the street, not knowing which way to turn. He wasn't ready to go back and look up at the windows there, or the door.

Surging around him, there was some indirection in the crowd as well. A gang of young teenagers, yelling, hammering street signs and kicking at a mailbox, was heading in the opposite direction to the family groups. Pierre saw them with indifference. Their exaltation was the direct result of beer, or the holiday mood, or the barometric pressure, or all of those factors. Had he ever been like that? It was not infectious now. He stepped aside and let them go by, then pulled the keys to the Chevette out of his pocket and held them in his hand. Was there anything he was supposed to do? Was it up to him to save Andrea? But she was already saved, or so she thought. I did not do this, he told himself. Yes, some things were his fault but not this.

He was still sure that he deserved more, that life had promised him more, that the unseen battle in the field had promised more. He was a lucky man who owned a house and miles of land. Surely setbacks and disappointments, betrayals, could only be leading to something better, to some ultimate reward or at least compensation. His brother had died when only a few weeks old but he, Pierre, had been granted life. He decided that the time had come for him to have a real drink. He shoved the car keys back into his pocket and followed the flow of people. Going through the rue Haut-Boc he met another gang of excited adolescents and, passing beneath a second-floor balcony, he overheard a woman up there as she leaned across to tell her neighbour that there were riots happening in Québec City. On television. *'C'est-u é-POU-vantable...!?'* she asked. Wasn't it DREADful? *'Ben oui,'* said the voice of the woman on the other balcony, complacently.

Pierre glanced up. For a moment he wanted to ask if they'd seen anything on the news about the hurricane that was supposed to be blowing up from the States, but from the way they looked down on him, he thought better of it. He turned the corner and let the crowd carry him along the rue Laviolette, towards the old town, the river and the rumoured fireworks. In front of the Palais de Justice, he changed his mind, cut across towards the rue Bonaventure instead and found himself outside the Café Zénob.

On a summer night like this, the Zénob was in its glory. Behind the heavy iron railings – salvaged, as most people knew, from Duplessis's collapsed bridge – drinkers crowded round the tables on the terrasse and overflowed onto the street, which had been closed to traffic. A small group of them was dancing to the thump of music from inside the bar and someone recognized Pierre. They called to him to join in but he refused. The dancers were mostly Zénob regulars, but others were holiday people who had come into town to gawk at the regulars. To them, the city centre was a different, wicked world. They stared. The scene did have a hectic quality. From his pedestal on the other side of the street the statue of Maurice Duplessis, wearing a slab-sided suit and holding a rolled document in his hand, looked down on them all. And over the heads of drinkers and dancers and onlookers, smoke and laughter wafted up into the leaves of the maple trees on the terrasse, their greenery translucent with strings of lights.

Pierre stopped when he saw that there in the crowd, at a corner table under the glowing leaves, was the girl with blue eyes. The lights from the tree cast a glittery shine on her hair and the clear whites of her eyes. Some of the tension inside him relaxed. Just by sitting there, she seemed to embody beauty and joy and liberty and hope and redemption. Looking at her, he felt a gust of relief, a homecoming at the rediscovery of so much youth and health and brilliant self-assurance.

When the girl smiled at him Pierre smiled back but kept going, down the steps and into the bar. As he passed her table, he heard her shushing her friends. They were talking about him. Well, he'd get to her later. First he needed beer, and not just one. He wasn't sure whether he'd eaten anything that day and he decided that beer was basically food. He plunged into the reassuring smoky din. There was after all more than one way of going back in time. His friends were here. At the back, he recognized Marc-André Malouin and a woman named Raymonde, looking sad as usual. Wasn't she with her poet boyfriend any more? He didn't speak to them. He couldn't remember the poet's name anyway. He was out of touch, but that could be remedied.

Pierre slid into his old spot at the bar and ordered a large Molson, which he swallowed immediately. Then he had another, maybe two or three others. He needed the anaesthesia to cleanse his brain. It wasn't easy to forget the feel of Andrea's bones under his fingers, or the unclean smell of her breath, and the mad light in her eyes.

Mistake, mistake, his mind yammered, should have seen it sooner, should have left her alone. At first the beer in his throat had a sorrowful flavour, the taste of defeat, of giving up. Drinking was what he'd been working hard at not doing. But then, quite soon, the sadness dissipated as his ideas began to repeat themselves with a sort of echo. Mistake. Left her alone. Never mind, the blue-eyed girl was outside. Nothing wrong with her. For the moment he couldn't remember her name but he'd get to her in due course. In due course. Nothing wrong with her. In the meantime, he smoked some of a joint someone passed to him. Any altered state of consciousness was better than remembering Andrea's eyes. Mad gleam. Sorrowful taste. Altered state. Soeur Surprenant might be in for a surprise herself, he thought. Surprise. Sorrowful.

After a while he asked for a double Scotch and carried it out to the table under the maple tree, where there was now a chair for him. Surprise. The blue-eyed girl was flanked by two others and they all smiled at him. However, there was still some difficulty in talking to her. The three girls faced him in a row and giggled to each other while he lit a cigarette and watched the smoke ascending into the lighted leaves above him. He persuaded himself that the clean-tasting Scotch was helping him to sober up after the beer and the marijuana. He rolled it around in his mouth. It was a disinfectant, it was medicine. Things seemed to be happening very slowly. Surely the other girls would leave. They always did. Girls understood that. But this time they didn't. The three of them sat there in a row smoking and watching him.

The result was that he found himself forced into something resembling a social conversation, asking the blue-eyed one what she was doing these days, if she was still at the Cégep When she said that she'd left the Cégep and had gone into a trade-school course, the other two girls tittered. What about? They were watching him. Well, if he had to make conversation, he would. He asked her what she'd studied. *'La technologie de la viande,'* she said, smirking. Meat technology.

At that the other two girls laughed loudly and kept their eyes on him, curiously. Meat technology. Well, let her explain. He waited, resting on the vapours of the liquor and staring up into the green.

The blue-eyed girl told him that she'd been studying to be a butcher. She'd learned to cut up and package animal carcasses for supermarkets. It was a field where there were jobs to be had and she was going to get one and then she was going to buy a car. She blew smoke at him.

Pierre tried to understand what he'd just heard. Was that really what she'd said? He considered the united phalanx of young females in front of him and wondered, for the first time, if he'd actually had sex with the blue-eyed one on New Year's Eve. It seemed unlikely. Meat technology. Surprise. And she had definitely been talking about him with the other two. There were undercurrents here. Undercurrents. And no reward. Had he done something he couldn't remember? Or was he remembering something he couldn't have done? Compensation. Retribution. But for what?

As he faced that triptych of unlined oval faces, they blurred and laughed with even rows of white teeth. They ran together into one smoky smile, then separated again. Take your chances, take your pick. They were all fantastically pretty, fantastically heartless. Pierre realized that it didn't matter if he couldn't remember the middle one's name. He was wasting his time. To them he was old. That was the problem. Nor could he drink as heedlessly as he once had. The alcohol had more effect now, and the effect, although lacking in the euphoria it had once produced, lasted longer. He swallowed the dregs of his drink and stood up, carefully. As soon as he turned his back on the three girls, they were gone from his mind. Instead he paused beneath Maurice Duplessis's statue, imagining something tentative in its pose, as if the Premier of Québec had found it tiresome to stand for the sculptor. Or was it that *le Chef* was ill at ease with the scenes he saw played out at his feet, night after night, on the terrasse of the Zénob? Pierre turned away.

By this time he had also forgotten about the fireworks but as he moved on down towards the rue Notre Dame and the river beyond it, he found straggles of people coming the other way. They looked tired and let down. Parents were explaining, disappointed children were whining. There had been no fireworks except for a few coloured rockets sent up from Sainte-Angèle-de-Laval on the other side. This year the town of Trois-Rivières had left its citizens free to build the traditional bonfires in their back yards but that was all. Did people even remember the custom? The mood of disappointment was familiar anyway.

Pierre continued down the slope, towards the St Lawrence. He noticed one jab of lightning and heard a perfunctory rumble in the darkness above the river but paid no attention. The American storm had obviously turned aside, it wasn't going to rain, and he had already won his gamble with lightning that day. He no longer hoped or cared. Night had laid its film of stale humidity over the weary grime of day but nothing else had changed, except that now he was drunk.

Soon after this it was past midnight, the holiday was over and it was already tomorrow. In the cooling air, the ordinary nocturnal business of the city was resuming. At the foot of the rue des Forges, the yard engine that moved giant rolls of paper from the warehouses along the waterfront to the various ships in port was halted, idling. During the evening's excitement, someone had parked a small car on the tracks and had not yet come back. Incongruously blocked by a cream-coloured Toyota, the locomotive chuffed and chanted its diesel song while a cluster of drunks discussed the problem. Call the police, said some, while others said no, why, come on, let's pick the car up, there're enough of us. And others yet, looking up at the dark cab of the engine, said no no, leave it, he's got a radio, a phone, something like that. He knows his job, he'll handle it.

Pierre ignored them. Drawn by the hypnotic rhythms from inside those riveted plates, he avoided the crowd and went around to the far side of the locomotive where he could listen at its towering metal flank. *Chuntle-chuntle-chuntle*, it sang and he leaned closer. In the dark where no one would notice him, he tried to analyse the structures of its music. *Chuntle-chuntle-chuntle*-CHUNTLE. He held his breath, wanting to understand, waiting to catch the sequence of the rhythms. Because there was order in it, there was a repeating percussive pattern. But just when he thought he had it, unexpectedly the engine paused and emitted an explosive sigh: PISSSHHHH-*tushhhh...!* Then *chuntle-chuntle* again. But still there was a composition there, not of tight compression, but of something relaxed, loosely organized and almost if not quite musically predictable. Almost alive. What Pierre heard in the diesel music was a powerful patience or humour, or maybe even compassion. He wanted to press his forehead against the riveted steel. He tried to measure the music off into bars in his mind but it was producing too many variations. Still, it offered comfort. Hidden within that flat, towering metal side was an affirmation of orderly life, an invisible pattern of intelligence.

But soon the owner of the Toyota arrived, at a run, and moved it off the tracks while the crowd applauded and whistled. The behemoth was freed and the diesel song accelerated to a whine, to a roar, to a blur. From somewhere – where? – came more thunder and Pierre found that he was clinging to the base of the steel ladder up the locomotive's side. The ladder moved. He was reluctant to let go but the mass pulled away and abandoned him. Suddenly respectful, suddenly aware of the thin and vulnerable flesh of human hands and feet, Pierre moved back from the colossal pressure of steel wheels on rails. And stood panting as the ponderous iron god, its dignity restored, clanged off into the tunnel under the Terrasse Turcotte. The boxcars rocked and pounded past him. By the time the last one had gone, the crowd had also vanished. Pierre was alone on the tracks. He turned to face the dark river. From above came another indifferent flash of lightning. Not even the cooling of night had brought rain.

He turned away from the port and started slowly up the wooden steps past the Terrasse Turcotte towards the Place de la Poste. With each step up, the air was a faint degree cooler. The steps themselves, built out of timber slabs like railway ties, were utterly solid and made no sound under his feet, but climbing them seemed endless, a repeated gesture that took hold of his mind and seemed to go on forever and ever. He floated up them, light-headed, in a sequence of movements that would never end, never arrive at the top. Then all at once he was at the top and the fascination of the steps was broken.

He looked around. There was one other person in sight, a teenaged prostitute who was coughing and shivering as she postured in tight shorts and a small halter top at the corner of the rue des Casernes. At Pierre she cast one brief glance and ceased posturing. Still coughing, she turned her back. He kept going.

In the square in front of the post office he came to the foot of a towering concrete monument in the stylized shape of a torch. *Le flambeau.* From its summit a gas-fed fire was throwing blue flames and yellow sparks up into the humid night. Pierre halted beside this, bewildered at how quickly everyone else had disappeared. The street was empty and the ragged light of the ceremonial flame was the only movement, its slight crackling the only sound. For a moment, from below the Terrasse Turcotte, there was also a chain of impacts, ordinary and unmusical, as the locomotive coupled another boxcar, then nothing more. The town was silent. Even the coughing girl had vanished from the corner of des Casernes. How had that happened? He hadn't seen a car stop, yet she was gone. While in solitary grandeur the flame above his head went on sizzling into the dark, heating nothing, burning for no apparent reason. Pierre saw again the little yellow fire at the centre of each of Andrea's eyes. He could no longer remember what the rest of her face looked like, only those eyes, her hunched silhouette and dragging feet, walking away from him and into some world of her own.

He shut his mind to her, trying instead to recapture the exact sensations of the invisible conflict in the field, the hot gusts of grunting and striking, the thud of bodies meeting or falling, the cool voids of retreat. That battle had been real and he knew that any uncertainty was solely in his perception of it. He'd had a momentary brush with another world. And now there was this blazing monument crackling above his head. He wondered if it was in commemoration of some war and how he had happened to miss that one too, whatever war it was. Meat technology. He stepped closer and bent to read the inscription written on the pedestal. Slowly following the carved letters around the curve, he learned that the flame had been visited in 1959, on the twenty-fourth of June, by Queen Elizabeth the Second. That struck him as amazing because it was the same date. And it was about the old Queen. Had she actually come here, to Trois-Rivières, in order to unveil an inscription saying that she had – what, come here? He shook his head, not sure he'd read it right. Farther around the pedestal he found another inscription, this one to in homage to '*la Petite Patrie*, 1634–1934'. And had the Queen read that part? In those days she would have been young and inexperienced, at any rate. Maybe they'd covered up the other inscription.

Pierre lifted his face to the flame, blazing twenty feet above him. Beyond it the sky was endlessly deep and black, the world was huge, the air dense and motionless as the inside of an enormous room. It seemed to him that he ought to know someone who had fought in a war but just for the moment he couldn't think of anyone. Unsteadily, with one hand on its concrete base, he continued to circle the flame, gazing dizzily upward. Three-quarters of the way round, he stepped into something soft, and looked down.

At his feet he found a bed of petunias, their colours pale in the firelight, their fragrance rising damply like a spicy fog. From far back in his drunken memory came a detail out of history. Marc Lescarbot had called tobacco *pétun*. Petunias were tobacco-flowers. Pierre smelled them better than he could see them, their scent recalling the essence of the girl with blue eyes, perfume and smoke wafting at him across a round café table. And with that he remembered at last how St John the Baptist had died. That burning-thin, desert-hardened prophet had been decapitated, sacrificed to the passing lust of a spoiled princess.

Pierre had a vision of his own head, blank-eyed and gory under the lighted leaves in the centre of one of the Zénob tables. Was that why the blue-eyed girl had laughed at him?

Because she thought it would be amusing to cut him to bits?
The nausea that had followed him all day surged up through
his body and he leaned over into the flowers, wanting to vomit,
but nothing came. Around his sacrificed head he distinctly saw
the circle of smoking girls, laughing, pouting, shrugging.
Tobacco flowers. When he straightened up again, the Place de
la Poste was swinging round and round.

In a rush of panic, he remembered his father, who had certainly fought in a war. His father who had known how to
plough and how to chop down trees. His father whose car he
had taken. For a moment he couldn't think where he'd left it,
his guilt obliterating the memory of his father's dying and
death, until his mind's eye gave him back the view of Andrea's
locked kitchen door with the car at the foot of the steps, and
then the picture of his mother's sad face and the stiff, shiny
shoes in her hand. Pierre found the keys to the Chevette in his
pocket. His car now. That's right, his father, who had survived
the war, had died this week. Pierre wondered why it was that he
himself had never experienced war. Had the invisible battle in
the field been his chance to fight? But how? There must have
been some failure of understanding on his part, some gap in his
knowledge of his family and his past. Tomorrow he would take
the time, he'd read some of those property documents which his
mother had had spread out on the table.

Then, for one illuminated instant, Pierre believed that he
could see through the texture of time, a semi-transparent trel-
lis-work of molecules, and down a black channel leading back
through the centuries. He closed his eyes and tried to envision
the face of the lost brother he had never known but saw only
lightning on the insides of his eyelids. He put out his hand to
support himself against the cement of the monument. Hadn't
there been something about a storm, a hurricane? He'd missed
that as well, missed all those palm trees laid out flat with their
fronds inverted and streaming like green flames into the wind.

There should have been rain. But no rain had come. Instead he was smelling smoke from somewhere else, not from the gas flame above his head. And he still had the tractor payments to cover and the ambulance bill. As well as miles of weedgrown land, overrun with unknown presences and waiting back there in the dark under the deep night sky. Waiting for him.

Pierre opened his eyes to look up at the sky and saw the flame. He supposed that the girl with the blue eyes might have used St John the Baptist's little lamb for a *méchoui*. Spitted and roasted the creature on the ceremonial bonfire because that was what she was trained for. What he was smelling was definitely woodsmoke. He laughed. But laughing, he reeled, and once more the scene revolved around him. He lost his balance and fell into the cool fluffy bed of flowers at the base of the monument. There seemed to be no reason to get up again, so he stayed there. Lying on his back amongst the petunias, with their soft trumpets brushing his ears and breathing fragrance into his face, he felt settled and connected. Above him the sky was a bottomless black ocean with a nexus of yellow fire flaring and crackling out from the centre in a circular shape like the mariners' compass. Flames surged to the cardinal points and fell back again. North, south, east, west. Back to north. From the outer blackness, beyond the flame, came one sharp cry from a night-flying bird. And from somewhere farther off, yes, there it was again, the faint smell of woodsmoke, because this was after all *la Saint-Jean*, even if there were no fireworks.

Ordinary people out there everywhere, in back yards up on the *coteaux* or along the river, were sitting in a circle around the big yellow blaze of the bonfire, enjoying the heat on their faces, drinking beer from the bottle and talking quietly about what they planned to do with their summer. Because it was summer now, that was what it all came down to. Summer. At last. How wonderful. And what did it matter if the girls at the Zénob had thought that forty-seven was old? He could learn, he *would* learn what his forebears had known. After all, some of them must have come out to New France from the very meanest streets of seventeenth-century Paris and they had learned, even through freezing winters and sweltering summers. Maybe some of them had been musicians and intellectuals too, but they had set their hands to the plough. It was a cycle, surely, like everything else, like painting the porch. Pierre closed his eyes to the light of the flame. He fell asleep.

And it wasn't until much later in the night, when even the flame, shut off by some automatic timer and valve, had suddenly shrunk and died away to nothing, and the silence really was perfect, that a water truck from the city works department stopped by the mass of flowers. Not noticing or maybe not caring about the dark blot of a sleeping man in their midst, it extended a slender, articulated metal arm with a hose and a nozzle attached to its underside. In a gesture of infinitely detached mechanical mansuetude, the nozzle flipped and turned down over Pierre and the petunias. Impartially, it watered them all with a gentle spray.

The Small Circle

Inside the tinted glass, Saskia kept her face down, away from her father. She stuck her riding crop down her left boot and scratched her ankle with it. She hated these rubber riding boots. They fitted her feet but were too short for her legs and too wide. They flopped. She needed leather boots. Proper people had leather boots.

She looked up resignedly as the car slowed. They were pulling into the stable yard. And then suddenly, incomprehensibly, everything was blank and blotted out. Saskia gasped. A hurtling mass of dark energy blurred, brushed the side windows of the big car and was gone again before either she or her father could understand what it was. It took them another two or three seconds to realize that a loose horse had nearly crashed into them. Then the animal had dodged aside and charged on out through the parking lot. Saskia forgot about her boots. Her father had yanked the wheel over hard but only after the danger was past. It was the horse that had avoided the car, not the other way around. By this time she could see that there were other horses out as well and when she saw the burst planks of the exercise ring, two thick horizontal bars smashed and hanging down, with the top rail gone completely, she knew what had happened.

Of course, a dark-coloured horse, it was the big bay stallion, their prize, their genetic champion. He'd crashed through the fence and rushed into the field after the mares. He'd burst the electric fence to get at them too, so that now there was no current to keep them in and they were running every which way.

There were horses out on the road and plunging through the neighbours' yards and gardens. Dogs were barking and people could be heard shouting, an accompaniment to the sounds of hooves hammering along the asphalt and in the distance, wood splintering.

Saskia's father snorted in disgust. Driving on into the yard he narrowly missed the stable cat, which was dashing for cover towards the *manège*, the indoor ring. For the cat, he stood on the pedal of his anti-lock brakes. He liked cats. And Saskia, flung against her seat belt, remembered noticing that he seemed able to feel tenderness for living creatures only when they were smaller than he was. He certainly despised horses. As for Saskia, fourteen years old and five feet eight inches tall, she no longer qualified for his affection either, if she ever had. He was only slightly more of a presence in her life now than when she was small and that was thanks to the divorce. Her father was supposed to visit her once every two weeks, and his bringing her to her riding lesson was the statutory visit. On alternate weeks she came in a taxi.

At the moment he was looking pleased at the scene of disorder and destruction around him. He maintained that horses were brainless organisms and he liked to say that natural selection would have eliminated them long ago were it not for adolescent human females who wanted to ride them. They were ludicrously overspecialized, he said, and of no further use in a world that had moved on without them. Destined for extinction. Naturally he'd never touched a horse himself and wouldn't have known what to do with one. He made a virtue of that fact and now he had the round-up on the road to confirm him in his contempt. He wheeled the car around and parked it.

He forbade Saskia to get out, so she had to sit in there with him, avoiding his eyes, seeing instead his hands on the wheel in a pair of pigskin driving gloves. They were new gloves and their leather smell filled the air-conditioned atmosphere inside the car. That summed him up, she decided, a pair of fancy pigskin gloves. While she wore rubber riding boots. Pigskin, she said to herself, skin of a pig, pigskin.

Gilles had told Réal that he shouldn't try to keep horses inside an electric fence because they moved too fast, but it was Réal's stable and he hadn't seen why not. He'd wanted to find out what was wrong with it his own way. Now he had. People were rushing past the car with lead-chains and halters, hoping to bring the mares back. The stallion wasn't caught yet and the next thing Saskia saw was the chunky grey gelding who'd been in the field minding the mares. He went puffing past and on out of sight. He wasn't about to be caught either. Réal ran down the road with a rope in his hand. There came more crashing noises followed by screams of equine rage. This didn't frighten Saskia, who would have liked nothing better than to get out of the car and go see what was happening. She knew that the gelding, the court eunuch, must have caught up with the young and crazy stallion. Now the two horses must be fighting and she was missing the spectacle. Instead she sat in the car, choking on the smell of freshly tanned glove leather.

Normally her father would have left by now. He never stayed for the lesson. He wouldn't have understood the commentary anyway – orders, criticism, encouragement, reproaches, and once in a while a grudging compliment – that Gilles shouted at her from the centre of the ring, because Saskia's father didn't understand French. That had been one of the lesser aspects of his marriage problems. French school for Saskia had originally been her mother's idea, even before she knew that the law required it. Her father's technique when anyone spoke French to him was to say 'Excuse me, what was that ... sorry...?' until the other person caught on and spoke English, as if French were some sort of misunderstanding or maybe a social blunder. He had even tried this with Gilles, but without success because Gilles had made not the slightest attempt to answer him. In

Gilles's world, English was simply inappropriate. It didn't work. So then Saskia's father had treated Gilles like a fool, assuming an attitude that seemed to imply that he himself was clever *not* to know any French, that it was somehow an interesting accomplishment, whereas an ignorance of English was a serious failing.

As far as Saskia was concerned, all this was pure humiliation. It was worse than the horse question. There was absolutely no one else in her world who could speak no French. How could he be so dense? A deaf-mute, she told herself, and without even sign language, it's amazing, he might as well be a deaf-mute, I have to interpret for him and he acts as if it's normal. Whereas nothing that Saskia had ever learned or been able to do was enough to win a word of praise for her from her father. He just wasn't interested.

His tense, impassive profile in the car and his gloved hands still on the wheel made it clear that he might have had better things to do with his afternoon. Once, three or four years before, when her parents were still trying to act married, Saskia had missed the school bus and had ventured to call him for a ride home. She'd been tempted to try it because she'd seen other girls calling their fathers. Therefore that must be normal, she had reasoned, even when deep down she had known that he wouldn't like it. But still she wanted to believe that she could do it too because that would make her like the others. And he *had* come to pick her up. In the car however he had informed her that he was not a taxi driver and that thereafter she was to make other arrangements or take public transportation. She still felt the guilt, especially now that he was driving her to riding lessons.

Saskia was old enough to understand that her father was simply bored with her. She'd had the time now to observe him and to consider the fact that he rarely talked to her at all unless circumstances made it unavoidable. Even here in the car, waiting for the horses to be corralled, he would scarcely look at her. And there was something else as well, something hinted at, grimly, by her mother. Somewhere, in some other, unthinkable dimension, he had what her mother called *lady* friends. Although her mother had not gone into detail, Saskia readily imagined the lady friends as smelling of perfume and having their hair treated by hairdressers, because these were practices that her mother had always scoffed at.

Saskia decided that late on a Thursday afternoon like this, if he hadn't had to bring her to her lesson, her father would have had a date. Maybe he had a date anyway. That was probably what he did during the three hours that he left her at the stable. Afterwards she knew that he would take her into town for dinner, would sit looking at her across a restaurant table for the rest of his duty visit, and then early in the evening would drop her off at her mother's house. The less time they actually had to face each other, the less awkward it was.

Was this her fault? Saskia never knew what to say to him. She supposed that he was ashamed to be seen with her in public because she was too big, not pretty enough, not well-dressed like the lady friends. Did people in fact understand that she was his daughter? That worried her. Moreover she hated her hair and was concerned about the shape of her nose. His open indifference made her feel ugly and stupid. Pigskin, she said to herself, staring out the car window and away from him, pigskin, pigskin.

Then she looked back over her shoulder and saw the stallion being led past the car by Réal and one of the stablehands. The horse was as beautiful as he was dangerous, a handsome dark bay, really a deep glowing brown colour shading to black at all his extremities. The faint dapples of his coat glinted like coppery facets as he struggled against the men holding him. They had two slip-chains on him, one on each side, and all three of them, the two men and the tall skittish horse with the flaring red nostrils, were jerking and prancing along together in a disordered sort of dance. The stallion was covered with lather and as he passed the car Saskia could see welts on his chest and bleeding bite marks among the *pommelures* on his glossy rump. The welts would be from the fence and the bites from the battle with the grey gelding.

At a safe distance behind them came Manon, one of the stable monitors. She was bringing the grey gelding back. Older and heavier and possibly smarter than the bay stallion, the gelding had apparently bested him in battle, because there were no marks on him. He was following Manon nicely, if at the same time snorting and waggling his head and generally looking pleased with himself. It had been fun but the performance was over.

Saskia glanced around and saw that Gilles had not participated in catching the horses. He was standing in the stable door, surveying the scene with contempt. He had that much in common with her father. But she supposed that he was also waiting for her. Their hour should have started fifteen minutes ago.

At last Saskia's father let her out of the car. He drove off and left her to her lesson. Unsure if they were actually ready for her, she hesitated between the stable and the *manège,* where the big doors were standing wide. Sometimes she could go straight in there to the ringside and find Titan already saddled because another girl had just finished her lesson on him. That was usually the easiest. That way she didn't have to saddle the horse. And Titan, a retired hunter, was the huge, quiet animal they mostly used for individual lessons. So she was just starting for the *manège* when Gilles stuck his head out of the stable and called her back. Today she'd be taking a horse from the stable, he told her. Then he vanished back inside and when she got there he was already in the stallion's box, tending to his injuries. Saskia waited. She knew what their priorities were.

Finally Gilles noticed her. Glancing over his shoulder, he told her to take Vapeur this time, from box number eight. Saddle and bridle number eight, he said, in the tack room.

Saskia felt a thrill of pleasure mingled with apprehension. She'd never ridden Vapeur. All she knew about him was that he was supposed to be a lot better than the big hunter. And although it was easy to take a scornful attitude towards a heavy, safe horse like Titan, he also inspired loyalty. He was a decent performer, he knew the rules, and she was used to him. Now Gilles had decided she was ready for a different horse. Saskia was flattered but not quite sure that today was the day she would have chosen for this new challenge.

However, one of their rules was that no one could question an instructor's decision. You rode the horse you were given. Saskia went to get the saddle and bridle, noticing that both were fancier and newer than what was provided for Titan. Girth trailing, buckles jingling, these she dragged around the corner and humped onto the saddle rack by box number eight. Then she rolled back the door and met Vapeur, a slender, anxious-looking brown gelding with a white face and one white foot. She put his halter on him and clipped the lead-chain to it. As she turned her back to lead him out of the box, he tried to take a bite out of her hair, but she felt his breath coming and thrust an elbow at him without turning around. At that, although she'd hardly touched him, he plunged sideways, running into the door frame and shaking the whole row of boxes with a booming crash.

That brought Gilles from the other side of the stable, immediately. Without speaking to Saskia, he grabbed the horse from her and attached him to the chains himself. Then he stood by and watched every move as she scraped out the animal's feet and brushed him down and saddled him. For Gilles, no buckle was ever well enough done up, no end tucked in securely enough – or the saddlecloth was too tight across the horse's withers, or the saddle was too far back – and besides she shouldn't let an animal reach out for her like that.

'Hit him on the nose,' he told her. 'We can't let them get away with that, these are school horses, children have to ride them.'

And Saskia was insulted. So Vapeur was another beginner's horse after all. Although she'd never had a horse of her own, she had been riding for three years and she was beginning to feel resentment at constantly being condescended to. Yes, sometimes she was nervous, and no, she was not yet a wonderful rider, but she was certainly not afraid of their school horses. She had noticed, in fact, that the stable people were more respectful towards girls whose fathers bought them horses and paid board, no matter how badly they rode them. Sometimes an ambitious daddy even bought a horse so highly bred that his daughter couldn't handle the beast at all. But then everyone would kowtow to her anyway, because she owned an Arab or an Andalou or an Appaloosa or whatever. Well, maybe not an Appaloosa. But Saskia knew that her father was certainly never going to buy her a horse, so at least she was not going to have to worry about being outclassed by an animal.

She reached for the bridle and looped the reins over Vapeur's neck while she undid the chains and removed the halter. Gilles stood watching. As Vapeur felt the chains come off, he pulled forward and lashed out at Gilles with a hind hoof.

At that, Gilles roared at the horse and seized him by the reins around his neck, then took the bridle out of Saskia's hands and hit the animal across the back with the full length of it, with the bit and other metal parts at the end of the swing. At once there was a great slewing and backing as Vapeur, all flattened ears and long yellow teeth, crouched and shrank in a clumsy grinding skid, his horseshoes striking sparks from the concrete floor. He looked fierce but all he wanted was to get away from Gilles.

Saskia moved out of the way, disgusted. This had nothing to do with her. She hadn't caused this. The horse was starting to sweat, long dark streaks appearing in the folds of his neck as Gilles brought him back into position, bridled him and threaded the martingale through the girth and the bit, doing up the buckles with authoritative little jerks. It occurred to Saskia that Vapeur was taking the brunt of Gilles's frustration with the stallion, left only temporarily to the ministrations of Manon, and that she herself might be able to reward this animal by being kind to him. But that couldn't happen until Gilles left her alone and went back to the more valuable horse.

Vapeur certainly didn't look very threatening. As soon as he felt the bit in his mouth, he underwent a transformation. Some switch clicked in his minuscule equine brain and he became the model school horse, dull and docile. His ears came forward, his nostrils ceased to flare and his head drooped. And as soon as the horse was calm, Gilles was also calm. He brought the reins forward over Vapeur's head and handed them to Saskia.

'Okay, take him into the *manège*,' he said. 'Make sure he goes through the door behind you, not beside you, don't let him get you up against the door frame again.'

Then he called to Manon to go with her, while he went back to the precious stallion.

Saskia wanted to tell Gilles that the horse hadn't had her up against the door frame for a single instant. She wasn't that stupid. Unfortunately, she hadn't got the words out before he was gone. And anyway, the main thing was to prevent Manon from actually taking the reins out of her hands. Manon was a tough little female, barely three years older than Saskia and several inches shorter. Her sole advantage was that she lived exclusively for horses and spent all her time at the stable. That made it easy for her to condescend to a younger girl who was still at school and who came, timidly, once a week for a riding lesson.

Sometimes Saskia wondered why she'd ever wanted to

learn. This sort of patronizing scene was not what she had dreamed of when she began. The horses of her childhood fantasies had been those mythic creatures of fire and velvet that were supposed to float through space without touching the earth, their only reason for existence being to embody the slightest caprice of human will and translate it into an effulgence of passionate action. Freedom, flight, power and beauty.

Real horses, unfortunately, were nothing like that. Instead Saskia had endured weeks and months and years of lessons on the wheezing, dragging, gut-rumbling *picouilles* that riding schools use for beginners. And if she was honest with herself, she had to recognize that, earlier in the season, Titan had in fact been a step up for her. She was making progress. Thanks to his stolid regularity, she had even acquired some understanding of technique. It was just that she had discovered no mysterious empathy with the beast at all. Nor did Vapeur, now tramping resignedly along at her elbow, give off any inspiring vibrations. These horses did not know or care what she longed for. They had already failed or finished somewhere else. Their feeble capacity for attachment to the human species, and whatever vestigial understanding they might have had of human reactions, had long since been blunted by the meaningless tuggings and kickings of beginners. All they wanted now was to get through with their uninteresting job and back into their boxes and resume chewing the wall or burping themselves against the edge of the manger. There was no freedom involved. Nothing was less free than a horse and the only real challenge here was dealing with Gilles and Manon.

Saskia reached the big doors of the *manège*, where Vapeur shuddered and hesitated. He stiffened his front legs, lifted his head and pulled a bit, but when she gave a little jerk on the reins, he followed her through without further resistance. There was nothing difficult about the horses. The challenge was the lessons. That was what she was forcing herself to face.

It wasn't fun but she was stubborn. Sometimes, not every time, they let her go out afterwards for a little trot through the woods. One day emancipation would come. Saskia hadn't given up.

Over the past few months she had learned more from Gilles than from any of her earlier instructors. Manon had let her know that Gilles was a Frenchman from France, from the French army riding school at Saumur, and Saskia soon found that he wasn't happy about teaching girls, because he didn't bother to be kind. Some of the others had even refused to continue their lessons with him, but Saskia didn't care about his attitude. No one had ever been very nice to her anyway. And although he shouted and insulted exactly as he had, presumably, with his cadets in France, she realized after a few sessions that her mother was paying for this and that she didn't have to take orders. Saskia was no military cadet. She could weep if she wanted to, and sometimes she did. She could give up, let go and slip off, and once or twice she'd done that. She could even refuse to get back on until the following week and sometimes she did that too. The first time Gilles had ordered her over a jump, she'd fallen hard from the top of it and had the breath knocked out of her. The following week, he had actually looked surprised to see her back.

But Saskia was going to keep at it until she learned. She still believed that there was a better understanding to be acquired, the secret of communication with the brute. Somewhere at the end of the tunnel there was a way out into the light, if only she could get past the leathery little man who stood in the centre of the arena, sneering and coiling his fifteen-foot lunge whip.

'Mais vous montez comme un pompier!' was what he'd yelled one day. That she rode like a fireman. Wow, thought Saskia, that must be really old school. And she wondered how long it had been since firemen rode horses, and what was so especially bad about the way they did it.

147

Now here she was again, standing in the sandy gloom of the *manège*, in the deep, simple odour of horses. How could this place smell of fear and comfort at the same time? But it did. She held Vapeur by the bridle while Manon supervised her, primly instructing her to lead the horse into the very centre and turn him sideways before getting on. He was co-operative and a lot smaller than Titan, so this was perfectly easy. Still Manon was all around her, saying don't do that, do it like this, don't grab the saddle at the back like that, you'll twist it, turn the stirrup more towards you, don't pull on the reins that way.

Oh, *Christ*, said Saskia to herself, practising under her breath to swear out loud one day. The horse was not tall and it wasn't that difficult for her to step up into the saddle. Once she was up, Manon told her that she should walk him around in the outer *piste* just to limber him up, and then she left. Saskia was alone with the magical animal at last.

He was much more malleable than Titan. He shifted sideways to a very slight knee pressure, and she experimented with that while there was nobody looking to tell her that she was doing it all wrong. She stopped and started him and trotted him a little. Compared to Titan, he was so responsive that he was wobbly. For once it was almost fun. He was narrow through the body and Saskia's legs had grown longer in the past year. She was relishing the feeling of being able to wrap her legs almost completely around the animal. She twisted her toes inward, wondering if she could touch them together under his belly. When she tried this he slowed down and stopped, so she let him stand while she leaned forward and scratched his mane just behind his ears. She knew they liked that. Maybe this one was actually a nice horse. He was obviously more sensitive than Titan. Maybe this one was the horse that would begin to fulfil her dream. His name was cute, Cheval-Vapeur, meaning horse-power.

Then she looked quickly over her shoulder to make sure

Gilles wouldn't come in and catch her petting him. You could never tell with Gilles. On rare occasions he would let the students do more or less what they wanted, letting them *discover* the horse he called it, but more often than not he got mad about nothing at all. Time and again he'd yelled at them for caressing a horse because, he reasoned, the animal hadn't done anything to deserve it.

'You congratulate them when they've jumped something or done something right,' he said, 'not just because *you* enjoy patting them!'

For the moment, however, Saskia and Vapeur, in agreement because there was no one to push or punish either of them, were happy just to stand there while she scratched his neck. The cat that her father had nearly run over came walking carefully down the bleachers along the side of the ring, then crouched on the fence and contemplated them both with round, assessing amber eyes. They'd be yelled at soon enough. Saskia took a deep breath and relaxed. Vapeur heaved a great girth-creaking sigh too, then swung his head and looked towards the entrance. Saskia turned in the saddle and saw why.

Gilles had just come in. He was striding down the length of the *manège* in an old grubby windbreaker with one torn shoulder, worn corduroy breeches and a pair of shining handmade boots that fitted his shanks like a leather skin. Heading for the far end of the arena, he told her that this week they'd be working in a small circle back there so as to leave the other end clear for Manon to walk the stallion and calm him down. Instantly Saskia felt the slight tingle of fear beginning again. That small circle business usually meant cantering, and she wasn't good at that. She had trouble controlling it. There was a point where a canter turned into a gallop, but where?

'Not with the stallion in here too? What if he doesn't like Vapeur? What if Vapeur's afraid of him?'

'No, no, don't worry about that,' said Gilles, 'that's a gelding you've got there, not a mare. No problem. And the stallion's tired out. Now walk Vapeur around in a circle for me. No, not like that. Shorten the reins. Come on, collect him. Sit back.'

Saskia tried this for a couple of circuits. She knew that she was supposed to hold the horse in and push him forward at the same time, but the way she did it was never right. Frustrated, Vapeur began to shift about, angling his rear to the wall and jerking his head. Gilles looked bored.

'*Ouf,*' he said, 'just stop pulling on his mouth like that and touch him GENTLY with both heels simultaneously and he should shift into a little trot.'

Saskia touched him as gently as she knew how, and he launched into a series of inefficient little well-bred buckings which made her laugh as she bounced along on top. Gilles always hated that.

'Too much!' he shouted. 'Too much! I didn't say to kick him in the ribs like that!'

Saskia slowed him down again. It seemed to her that she'd hardly touched him. She could hear Gilles lecturing her about the difference in riding horses with *blood*. Blood? Didn't all horses have blood, anatomically? Better not to ask. While Gilles talked on she arrived at the proper dynamics to get a small trot and trotted round, hoping for approval. She sat the horse rigidly, trying to maintain the correct position, holding him back with the bit and nudging him forward with her legs, carefully. The worst problem was trying to do everything she was told and ride the horse as well. Round and round they went. Sardonically, Gilles watched, coiling his long whip. Saskia was far more afraid of the lunge whip than of the horse. Then Gilles got down to business.

'Okay,' he said, 'now move your left knee forward a bit. Pull your right leg back. ADVANCE your left leg. Right. Lower your hands. Shorten the reins more ... MORE. And even them up, can't you see the outside rein is too long? Why do you think his head's crooked like that? Push him with your legs and hold him in with your hands. But DELICATELY! Don't jerk like that. Sit back. And don't let him out too much. Come on, shorten him.'

The horse was tenser now and beginning to pick up his feet. Saskia enlarged the circle and started along the wall, riding away from the doors where Manon and the bay stallion would soon appear. She did try to keep her left knee forward and her right knee back but it was hard to know if she was succeeding, since she couldn't even keep her bottom in the same place for two impacts.

'Okay, NOW!' shouted Gilles. 'In the corner! *Galop!* Touch him at the girth with just your left leg and open your hands!'

Saskia did try to do all this but there was no canter, no gallop. Anticlimax. Vapeur simply trotted faster, and not in a very round circle. Not collected enough, she supposed. Maybe she hadn't tried hard enough. She was also expected to give a suggestive thrust with her pelvis, with her whole body, as she touched his side and opened her hands. She hadn't done that. Well, it could hardly have any effect when she was barely in contact with the horse. But she wasn't going to do it either, not with Gilles watching every move. Understanding was enough. She'd do it right later, when she got the horse alone, if ever. When she'd at least learned how to maintain contact with the saddle.

While Gilles was already yelling at her, 'No, no, not like *zat!* Shorten the reins more. *Mais non! Pas comme* ... not like *zat* ...'

Sometimes, in the heat of his instructions, Gilles got so excited that he even tried to speak English to her. The implication was that she couldn't understand his French properly, which never helped. And in whatever language, his voice would finish by coalescing into a hypnotic jabber, running on and on, too hard to listen to while she was struggling to understand the horse as well, floundering along on the heavy, dim-witted beast that was her fellow victim, her partner in confusion. Vaguely, she knew that the bay stallion was in the ring now too, at the other end, being walked round and round. Out of the corner of her eye she saw his red blanket, and she saw Manon watching her lesson. She saw the cat as well, still sitting on the fence, observing the action. As she bounced past, beginning to feel out of breath, he yawned daintily, displaying pointed white teeth and a curled-back pink tongue. But Gilles was yelling at her again.

'Don't look round like that, you distract the horse, look where you're going, DEFINE where you want to go ... Vapeur looks where you look ...'

Saskia knew that where she wanted to go was out into the woods, to the sunlight and the leaves and the vistas of the real world. She would have liked to walk this harmless, helpless animal along a quiet trail, to let him eat grass even, to listen to the sounds of the trees with him, to smell the earth and the vegetation, and to try to perceive reality through the simplifying lens of his uncomplicated apprehensions. Maybe there she'd trot a little, maybe even gallop in the direction going away from the stable. She imagined doing it perfectly, flexing and bending so that she stayed with the saddle, moving her legs to the correct angle, opening her hands and *lifting* the horse into a gallop. That was what it was called in novels. She'd never experienced it. But for now it was enough to know what to do, she didn't have to show Gilles, she had nothing to prove to him. He was still remonstrating.

'Don't pull like that on the inside rein ... that's not how you make a circle. Yes, *enfin* ... *Non!* I want you to tighten the *outside* rein to hold him in a clean curve, it's the opposing pressures that do it!'

By now her father would be where? The pigskin gloves on the steering wheel. She wondered if he might be in a cocktail lounge somewhere. Saskia had never been inside a bar but she imagined a darkly mysterious place with velvet furnishings, deep chairs and small lights, everything redolent of cigarette smoke and aftershave lotion and the slightly acid smell of men's bodies through layers of dry-cleaned clothing. Usually on these afternoons her father would come back smelling of alcohol, and she knew now what the smell was. When she was little, she'd taken it to be a part of the mysterious odour of the grown-up man, an essence which she associated with freedom, importance, prestige, and clothes from the dry-cleaners. The smell of a suit. Her mother, who had never actually mentioned the bars, had often protested at his extravagant use of the dry-cleaners. Saskia wondered about that for the first time. Was it because of lipstick stains or something else to do with women? She tried to imagine her father touching someone. He never touched her at all.

'No, no, too much! You're dragging on his head for nothing! You hold him into the circle with your legs and your body and you RESTRICT that with the outside rein. Stop!'

Gilles came over and grabbed her leg and her boot and showed her where to put her foot, how to angle it. He held the horse with one hand and her leg with the other, turning it, forcing the heel of her boot against the animal's ribs. Vapeur jerked forward when he did that but Gilles stopped him with one hand. Then Gilles let go, stepped into the centre and ordered her back to the circle to try the canter again. Saskia still hadn't managed it even once. She didn't believe that it was really possible. Nothing this big could gallop in such a small space. She and Vapeur went labouring around at a trot again, working against each other.

'*Des jambes, des jambes!*' Gilles was howling at her. Legs, legs!

It seemed to Saskia that Gilles put his hands on her legs and thighs a lot more often than was strictly necessary for the purposes of the lesson. He ran his hands over the horse and, when he came to the girl sitting on top, his hands simply kept on going. Saskia was very slightly pleased about this and at the same time, mystified. Gilles was physically smaller than she was, and married, and in his forties. He couldn't possibly be interested in her, it was inconceivable. But for a few moments she wondered about his life, if he hated his job, if he ever just wanted to go for a ride in the woods alone. She wondered if he actually liked horses.

And then she wondered about his body, about the tensile toughness of him. Although he was smaller than she was, she had seen, often enough, what he could do with a horse. Once she'd seen even Titan trembling and flaring his nostrils. That was on a day when the big horse had innocently dumped some hopeless learner, only to find that Gilles was on his way over to straighten him out. Poor honest hardworking Titan, Gilles had then made him take a big double jump at a gallop, over and over, and in both directions until he was completely blown.

It occurred to Saskia that when Gilles had been unable to communicate with her father, he hadn't apologized or seemed to care. He'd simply lifted his chin and waited for her to explain what the man wanted. And she thought about the fact that Gilles had been an officer in the French army. She wondered who was really tougher, Gilles or her father.

Saskia didn't see the lunge whip coming, but she knew when it must have flicked Vapeur's hocks, because suddenly he leapt forward into a gallop. For an instant she went completely blank. And after that she saw nothing but a fountain of mane erupting in front of her. All she could do was hang on. Her floppy boots slipped and folded and a fold pinched her leg. But she couldn't worry about that now. The stallion! she thought. Where is he? There was no question of any circle now, as they plunged down the length of the *manège*. Then for a flash the cat was in front of her, leaping down from the fence.

And the horse just dropped out from under her. There was

no time to worry about falling. This wasn't like losing her balance and slipping off over the shoulder, this was an explosion. Another blank, and she was lying in the sand with a confusion of flying filth and hooves coming down all around her head. She heard Gilles's voice shouting at her not to move. She didn't. She couldn't anyway, because she couldn't breathe and she couldn't see very well. But gradually the ceiling of the *manège* came back into focus and she sat, then stood up, trembling and dirty, but not hurt. She tried taking an uneven, gasping breath. Yes, her lungs worked, she could breathe again. The worst of it was knowing how much Manon enjoyed seeing her come off.

She looked around. The stallion, still in his red blanket, was twisting and snorting while Manon tried to soothe him, glaring at Saskia at the same time. By losing control and charging out of the circle she'd frightened the expensive high-strung beast, already traumatized by earlier defeat. Another of their rules was that it was never the horse's fault. And the most important rule of all was that she had to get back on, right away. Gilles, smirking, had gone to catch Vapeur for her. Vapeur recoiled and rolled his eyes at him but Gilles said nothing as he led the horse into the centre and held him for her. When she turned the stirrup and grabbed the saddle, Vapeur nipped at her, and this time she did hit him on the nose. On top once more, trembling – but the horse was trembling too – she picked up the reins.

'Now,' said Gilles, laying a hand on her knee, 'do you know what you did wrong?'

'No ...' she said, distracted by the pressure of his hand. She noticed how large it was, considering how small he was, and through the stretch fabric of her breeches she could feel the heat and hardness of it.

'You always fall off when you're too far forward, I keep telling you to sit *back*. Get your weight back and the horse out in front of you and you control him. No one ever falls off over the rump. What did you expect when you were hunched over his neck like that?'

'Yes, I see,' said Saskia humbly.

Secretly she thought of rodeo clowns who did fall off over the rump – but was that just because it was difficult to do? Anyway, Gilles wasn't telling her anything she didn't know. It was simply that her reflexes didn't know yet. And his hand was still there on her knee.

'... and remember that this is just an animal. YOU'RE responsible for what happens. It was up to you to remember that there was a cat sitting there and to think ahead to what might happen. Why didn't you?'

'I ... was afraid of the stallion ...'

'Afraid of the stallion! Look at him! What is there to be afraid of...?'

Saskia heard Manon sniggering as she led the dappled bay horse along the wall past them. Manon threw open the big doors at the end of the *manège* and escorted him out, his long red robe swishing preciously against his thin black legs.

'... it wasn't the stallion you should have been afraid of. Now, listen to me, you're supposed to create the impulsion and then control it. But you weren't creating any impulsion. So I used the whip to give you that impulsion and what did you do with it...?'

Saskia remembered that she was still supposed to have supper with her father afterwards, her opulent, untouchable father in his white shirt, his impeccable suit, his pigskin gloves. And now she had manure in her hair, she'd stink up the restaurant. While he was fresh from some sophisticated girlfriend, probably. He was going to like her even less than usual.

As she told herself that she didn't care, and as Gilles's voice continued, the cat reappeared from under the bleachers, slightly ruffled, and started out across the sandy wastes of the ring. Ignoring the relentless voice, feeling the horse calming under her, Saskia watched him go. For a feline, he'd had a strenuous day too, nearly run over, nearly trampled. But no one worried about a cat. Cats were taken for granted in stables and had to take their chances. People petted them in passing, then went off to deal with all the medical and behavioural problems of their hypersensitive equines.

This cat was a fluffy ginger-coloured animal, too long-haired for a dirty place like a riding ring. He wasn't very clean. Distractedly, Saskia noticed that he was crossing the space diagonally, following the first trajectory of the path that a horse would have taken in describing a figure eight. He was aiming not quite for the back corner, but for one horse-length short of it. As she watched, he altered his course and did head directly for the corner.

Manon had left the end doors of the ring standing open and now, from that direction, over Gilles's words, Saskia thought she could also make out the stealthy crunching sound of her father's car arriving, its fat Michelins turning in the yard outside. The big car's engine made no sound at all but she could imagine the tires, their smothery vulcanized viscosity bulging down to espouse and crush the gravel – power muffled, gloved and shielded, turning in its own tight circle. She actually shuddered and the tired horse, not understanding what the tremor meant, perhaps expecting punishment, flinched beneath her. Saskia knew, however, that her father wouldn't come inside. She could be sure that he'd stay in the car until she came out. He wouldn't want to dirty his shoes or risk having French spoken to him. The *manège* was Gilles's territory. As these things travelled through her mind, the cat continued to pick his way, delicately, through the churned-up sand and manure.

'… okay,' Gilles was saying, 'there's no point in insisting on it any more for today.'

He lifted his hand from her knee.

'Just take your feet out of the stirrups and walk him around in the outside *piste* on a long rein for a few circuits. Next week we'll work on the *épaule en-dedans* ...'

Saskia felt as if she might faint, her ears ringing, still hearing Gilles's voice droning on, but from farther and farther away. Her mind could no longer tune in for as much as a full sentence. She had been hoping to be allowed to go off into the trails this time, but Gilles hadn't offered that and now her father was back, so she focused again on the ginger cat. He was the only living creature here with any real freedom. As she watched him, he reached the far corner of the ring. Fussily, he circled the ground, inspecting it. He chose a spot and scooped himself out a nice deep hole. He sniffed it several times and inspected it from various angles. Then he turned his back to the horse and the lesson, to Saskia and to Gilles (who was rolling up the lunge whip), adjusted himself over it, stretched out his tail, and proceeded to shit in it with accuracy and disdain.

Saskia felt a dizzy longing to laugh but didn't dare while Gilles was still standing there. He might not think it was funny if she pointed out to him that the *manège* was quite a bit like a gigantic cat box, so she sat motionless, primly holding the reins, her knees in and her heels out, with her knuckles properly turned down on the horse's neckbone, waiting for Gilles to go. At last he did. As his silhouette disappeared through the doors, the cat looked around. He glared back across the sand in her direction. Then Saskia did pull her feet out of the stirrups. She let her shoulders slump and she forgot all about how she was supposed to hold the reins. She let them run out through her fingers and hang in two long loops on either side of the horse's neck. Letting her feet dangle, she gave a small thrust with her body and Vapeur started obediently along the wall. Now she had only to lean with the slightest inclination and he turned and plodded in a perfect circle. At a walk like this it was easy.

At last she could relax. She flopped forward, laid her face on the horse's neck beside his mane, and let him continue, round and round, as a wave of calm, of profound relief, flooded over her. Her cheek stuck a little to Vapeur's sweaty hide, then unstuck as, with each step, her cheekbone received the jolt of the leg and shoulder, the long rigid bony structure meeting the ground, stiffening, folding, meeting the ground again. Clomp, clomp. Such big bones. Such thick neck muscles. The slick hairs of his mane were coarse too, stiff and shiny under the gummy deposit of dust on sweat. Everything about these animals was on such a large scale and at the same time so vulnerable. To the best of their limited abilities, most of them did what they were told. All decisions, all responsibility, were left to the human rider. Saskia rolled her face away from the sticky horse odour of his mane and put her ear against his neck. Now she could not only hear it, she could feel the big slow heart pumping that blood that Gilles had wanted her to appreciate.

Thoroughbred blood of course. And in fact she did know what he'd meant by blood. Vapeur must have some thoroughbred in him. But he wasn't all that excitable. Would that just be because he was old – fifteen or sixteen? Saskia wondered what failures in his career – what losses on some third-rate racecourse – would have brought him down to giving lessons at the end of his life.

Horses only lived to be about twenty, she knew that, and as the jar of each hoof set down was transmitted up the leg to her ear, she thought about it. If he had stepped on her today, Vapeur could easily have killed her, yet despite the density of his bones and skin and hair, despite his huge heart and lungs, his long stride, he was going to wear out in just a few more years. Whereas she, Saskia, with her frail human bones, her snub nose, frizzy hair and short square hands, was quite possibly good for another seventy or so. In fact Vapeur might be dead before she had even finished growing up.

I'm going to outlive them, she thought, not just this poor horse, or the stallion, who's only five, but Gilles and my father too. I'm going to outlive them all. So there's time. For whatever it is that I have to do with my life.

Vapeur came to the corner where the ginger cat was busy covering his deed and Saskia, still lying on the horse's neck, looking down his leg, stopped him when she saw yellow fur moving prudently out of the way of the hooves. The cat looked up at her and she spoke to him.

'I'm not that hopeless, you know,' she said. 'I am learning.'

The cat blinked.

'You're only a cat,' she said to him, 'but you're a survivor too. Like me. Nine lives. Even if we're both a bit grubby.'

It occurred to her that the cat might have used up most of his nine lives by now. And suddenly, unexpectedly, there were hot tears welling up through her sinuses, running over her face and down into Vapeur's mane, mixing stickily with his sweat. With no other human present, Saskia gave in to the luxury and wept. Vapeur didn't seem to mind. Saskia wailed while he sighed, let his head droop and waited. But the cat stared at her for a only second or two, sobbing into the horsehair, switched his tail twice and skulked off. Human distress, so what. Saskia closed her eyes, then opened them again. She took a deep breath.

'Live and learn,' she said, to herself this time.

She unstuck her face from the horse's neck, straightened up, snuffled back her tears and, still holding the reins, wiped her cheeks with both wrists. Then she put her feet back into the stirrups, heels down, shortened the reins and nudged the horse out of the trampled circle. She rode him down the *manège* towards the open doors. The white daylight striking in through the bars of dust made her eyes water again and she wept a few more tears in spite of herself. Out there, they were going to notice that she'd been crying, but she tried not to care. She could always let them think that it was just shock. Because after all she had fallen off the horse.

Laiah and the Sun King

Sunk in his lawn chair, his glass of rosé held by its stem in his dry, elegant old fingers, the Greek poet tugged the flaps of his leather coat across his knees with his other hand. Surely October was late in the season for a garden party, even on a smoky golden day like this one. The sunlit air was an illusion. It barely warmed the surfaces of wood and stone and concrete, while up from the grass, from the ground beneath it, from the damp deep gritty earth, there radiated the solid chill of impending frost. In such a cold country, couldn't they have been invited into the house? The Greek poet was unceasingly aware of the big brick house at his back. He longed for its inner spaces. Its very bricks, deep red in the sunlight, gave off a faint, frustrating glow of warmth, hinting at heat and comfort. The Greek was too old for these junkets, too old to travel to northern countries and stay in strange hotel rooms and be forced to sit outside on a cold flimsy chair listening to the self-serving chatter of other poets.

However, the festival organizers had made such a point of inviting him, even sending the two airline tickets, that he had been unable to refuse. It was too good a chance to pass up. The Trois-Rivières festival was starting to be recognized internationally. And although the Greek poet did entertain grave doubts about the possibility of really translating poetry, he knew that his French was good and that the French versions of his own work happened to be excellent, for translations. Last night the Québec public had listened in a way he had never known before. After a long career of intermittent recognition, intermittent glory, he was now successful, but nonetheless had found that respectful silence in the crowded, dizzying restaurant, and the applause that followed it, profoundly moving. If only the memory of it could warm him now. But at least his poems had been heard and his name had been published. They told him that he had even been seen on television. And he had sold a dozen books. Therefore these discomforts had not been in vain, and perhaps he could endure them for a little longer.

There was more than that. The Greek revolved the wineglass in his fingers as he watched the others on the lawn. Life had been hard enough and often empty when he was young. That he had not forgotten. The result was that now, in old age, even if sometimes he found life too full, too demanding, he also felt that it would be foolish to refuse any prospect of happiness when the time remaining was probably so short. Today, here, now, he was especially happy, because they had made it possible for him to bring Laiah with him and she was having a wonderful time.

She didn't seem to feel the cold. He watched her as she negotiated the lawn with delicate, deliberate steps, smiling at everyone around her. Then he shivered. A current of cool air had come from behind, feathering his hair and carrying scraps of conversation. With another part of his mind, he listened to what was being said. '*Teez-awl...?*' asked a resonant Middle-European voice. That was the voice of a young Serbian poet. He was one of those whom the Greek had met at the restaurant last night, when they'd read together for the television camera. '*Non, non,*' said the other voice, closer, a British voice, he thought. '*Tee-sol, T.E.S.O.L.*'

The Greek knew only a little English but could identify its dragging diphthongs and the clumpings of a tonic accent in the Englishman's French. '*C'est veut dire ... pour enseigner à les gens qui parlent, qui ne parlent ...*'

164

The man's French was weak. He wasn't sure of communicating what he meant. His lawn chair creaked tensely. He must be leaning forward. Now he'd fallen back into English, speaking very slowly and clearly.

'It stands for ... the teaching of ... *English* to speakers of *other* languages. Our new programme ...'

Looking into his wine, the Greek drew in a longer breath of the bright chilly air. He studied the rose-gilt glints of sunlight on the cold surface of the pink liquid. He took a sip. It was too cold for him to taste it properly and he held the glass away from him again. As for the Englishman behind him, he recognized the type, the language teacher. They were everywhere. Somehow this one had made his way to Québec, and on an autumn afternoon found himself in Trois-Rivières. Someone must have invited him to this garden gathering to meet the poets from the festival, maybe because he had announced himself as a translator. Now he was using the occasion to explain the advantages of learning English to the Serbian poet. Well, that was fine, *de bonne guerre*, as they said. Probably the two behind him understood each other well enough.

The Greek already knew that the young Serb had arrived in Québec by way of Paris and could speak nothing but Serbo-Croatian and a little French. He had not yet published a book. He was carrying his poems in his briefcase, a mass of loose sheets, some in Serbo-Croatian and some in hasty, heavy French translations. He was young and keen, and he was especially eager to find a second-stage translator, from French into English. As for what might remain of his original poems after two successive translations, evidently the Serb didn't realize or didn't care. The Greek, sitting a few feet from him, could read his mind. All he really wanted was to get away from the war. After all, this was America, he had set foot on the North American continent for the first time three days before, and he was determined to move on into English. He was a poet, not a soldier, and the war was behind him, to be mentioned by him only with scrupulous detachment, although it was present in the minds of all who heard him read. The Serbian poet was perfectly sure that one day, through the powerful international medium of the English language, he would be a great success, famous even. That would be why he was straining to understand the T.E.S.O.L. man. Was he even really a poet? The Greek poet swirled his wine. The very literal translations that the Serbian poet had read on the previous evening didn't show it. But that didn't prove anything. To the Greek poet, old and famous and secure, it was only a little depressing to wonder if the Serb might be one of the sincere fakes, a simple poetaster. And how did one define imposture anyway, if the man was entertaining? Was poetry an intellectual display, or was it performance art? What was true was that the Serb passionately wanted to be a poet and not a soldier. That was all that mattered. Now the pair behind him had fallen silent. No doubt they were also watching Laiah as she advanced down across the lawn towards the view. People usually stared at her.

Looking past her, what the Greek poet saw was the view down and away over the escarpment, across the lower, western part of Trois-Rivières. Over the edge and below the lawn there stretched a neighbourhood of humble duplexes and two-storey apartment houses, for a while yet still gilded with autumn sunlight. Off to the north was some sort of industrial sector and in the other direction, to the southwest, loomed the criss-crossed girders of an enormous bridge, lunging along the horizon and, he supposed, across the St Lawrence River, which could not itself be seen. Yes, that must be the big river because an ocean-going ship was coming into view. Its superstructure glided along the ragged line of roofs and treetops and gradually melded its design to the iron lines of the bridge. Steaming through underneath, it provided brief spatial reference. Otherwise the clean geometric arc of the bridge defied perspective.

From moment to moment, the Greek, with his long-sighted eyes, imagined it angled away from him, then towards him. Both interpretations of the vision seemed convincing.

And Laiah, there was Laiah still advancing across the lawn with her hand extended, perhaps for it to be kissed by someone, perhaps simply for balance. Laiah could make a life's work out of crossing a lawn. Her heels sank into the earth and her legs, slightly swollen in shiny tight stockings, wobbled along past a border of chrysanthemums, their mass of rusty pinks and golds backlit by the sinking sun. Beside the flowers, the host of the party, also a poet and eighty years old himself, was explaining to a woman whom the Greek had not met that he had planted them forty years earlier. He was a slender man with thick wavy white hair, a noble head, articulate hands.

To live alone in such a house, thought the Greek, and with a garden. But so cold. The white-haired poet had ushered his guests straight through his library and out onto the lawn. The Greek had caught only a glimpse of the interior. Meanwhile the eighty-year-old poet was gesturing towards his chrysanthemums with one of those long hands, as elegant as the Greek's own.

'They bloom until December,' he was saying.

But the Greek poet, unable to stop shivering, was thinking of the plate-glass window behind him and longing for the panelled interior on the other side of it. He had seen walls of books in there, and upholstered armchairs and warm carpets. Central heating, they always had central heating in this country, why sit outside? Then he observed that Laiah was in fact making her way towards the edge, the place where the lawn dropped off.

A tall, heavy man was standing there on the crest of grass at the end of the garden, gazing out at the view and over the yards, presumably, of the working-class dwellings beneath the escarpment. This was a man only in his forties with an aquiline nose and straggling blond hair waving against his round cheeks and fluttering over his collar. While the others were watching Laiah, he seemed not to have noticed her. His pose, in black jeans, a black polo shirt and a tweed jacket with its collar turned up, was Byronic, chin lifted. As the Greek studied him, he lowered his eyes to something below him and over the edge of the grassy verge, something which none of the others could see. Still turning the glass by its stem, his wine an immobile puddle within the circle of its containment, the Greek then saw the man in black reacting, taking an interest and stepping closer to the edge. Whereas Laiah hadn't reached him yet. She had paused beside the chrysanthemums where their host was turning to speak to her.

The Greek knew her age but kept her secrets. What could the casual observer know? Was she fifty-five, seventy-five or perhaps even older? The flesh of her face had been tugged tightly upward, probably more than once, so that her jaw was weirdly fleshless but not exactly sunken. Her teeth and all the bones of her mouth were too prominent. Her dragged-back eyes were painted up at the corners in bold black strokes which reached to her stretched eyebrows. The frail fizz of her teased hair, a matte black, stood out around her narrow skull, quivering in the cool air. She had a small protuberant belly and wore a short, narrow black skirt and a black suede jacket with black mink tails hanging off the shoulders. Officially she was or had been Russian, and was possibly also Jewish. He had first met her in Lisbon, after the war. They had been together for most of the decades since. But even the Greek poet, who had long been her lover, did not know everything that Laiah had seen in her life, what she had endured, what she had escaped, what survived. There was so much that she would never tell. She was simply Laiah, her own creation.

Shrinking in his leather coat, not drinking his wine, he contemplated her beside the flowers, not really able to imagine what their host must be seeing as he looked at her but tempted, briefly, to speculate. Surely a man who lived among all those books, yet who also planted flowers, would perceive the essential Laiah. What the Greek poet saw in her ancient eyes was centuries of femininity. Laiah projected a faith in beauty, in the notion of the beautiful as an absolute and of the self as precious – such wise and fragile strength. And in the final analysis, he knew that what others thought or might think of her was of no importance to him because she was his.

He stared back down into the cold wine in his glass. It was a pale golden rosé, *grain de gris*, almost the colour of the chrysanthemums. Having tasted it once, he settled for admiring the colour. He lifted the glass and held it against the sky, looking into it like a crystal ball, trying to remember if Laiah had been beautiful when he first met her. She had been very hungry then. To him she seemed most beautiful now. Through the wine's wobbling refractions he viewed her legs and stockings and the row of flowers, his fingers slowly numbing as he held his glass aloft. And he continued to long for the unexplored comforts of the big house at his back. A garden party in October. In such a climate.

Behind him meanwhile, the Serbian poet, in slow, thickly Slavic French, was labouring to establish a contact, to find some common acquaintance. *'Vous connaissez? Elle s'appelle ... euh ... Julie ... oui, Julie ... euh ... McCeuh ..., Mc ..., McGee ... je ne sais pas trop. Une dame qui fait article sur guerre en Bosnie, elle est à Montréal, vous connaissez...?'* 'Yes...?' said the English specialist. 'McGill?' *'C'est ça, McGeel, elle fait traductions. Vous faites aussi traductions?'* 'Translation? At McGill? Well, of course I'm not ... our programme isn't ...'

Still halted in her progress towards the blond poet, Laiah was admiring the chrysanthemums with their host, who continued to look closely, curiously at her. And the blond man who, the Greek now remembered, was a Montréal poet and fairly well known, had stepped down out of sight over the edge of the lawn. He'd seen something down there that interested him. The Greek had already decided that this man was possibly homosexual, or at least bisexual. That quality might well be what was attracting Laiah to him. The Greek knew her well and smiled secretly into his own reflection in his wine. One of the reasons he was a poet was that there had always been things he knew without being told. The crown of the Montréal poet's golden head could just be seen above the edge of the lawn as he walked across towards the other side.

And over the edge, what the blond poet had been drawn to — and what the Greek did not need to see — was the tableau of a man, in the shadowed yard below, who was working on his car. This man, in jeans and a work shirt, had come out of his house in a wheelchair and had crawled out of that and up onto the engine of a large old car. He was sprawled across the air filter, working with a wrench, twisting with his powerful arms at something underneath him, while his legs trailed off over the fender. As the blond poet stared, the man heaved himself farther over and settled right into the engine, sitting on some part of it, while his wheelchair, tilted and abandoned, remained propped beside the passenger door. After a few minutes he crawled back onto the fender and flipped himself into the chair, where he lit a cigarette. He dragged on that and glared at the car.

That was when Laiah appeared behind the Montréal poet and above him. He hadn't seen her yet, but she was also looking down at the man in the wheelchair. And she stopped, glancing from him to the Montréal poet and back. When the man below looked up and saw them both watching him, he threw his cigarette onto the gravel. He scowled and wheeled himself around to the driver's door of the car, slid in, dragged the folded wheelchair after him and slung it over his shoulder into the back seat. He slammed the door while Laiah, unsteadily, was trying to descend the slope to the blond man. When she tried this her mysterious agelessness vanished. She was a very old lady and the angle was too steep for her. She must have made a little sound because the Montréal poet turned and saw her. She was falling and he reached out and caught her just as the repaired car was turned on with a shuddering roar. There was a lurch, then a cloud of demonic black smoke as the crippled man inside backed it out onto the street below. '*Oh, merci, excusez-moi,*' said Laiah in the arms of the Montréal poet.

She would have said more but her words were covered by the squeal of wheels as the car was slammed loudly into drive and took off, fishtailing round a corner and out of sight.

From the other end of the garden, even the Greek poet heard its ragged combustion, and then he saw Laiah in the clutches of the Montréal poet as he helped her climb back to the lawn, the pair of them aureoled against the sinking sun as they emerged over the grassy edge of the earth. He saw the blond man lead her back past the chrysanthemums. The powerful portly figure with the cruel profile and the gleaming hair held her gripped firmly by the arm so that her high heels and swollen legs flowed past the dry-looking flowers without seeming to carry her weight. Her feet moved and she was transported almost without touching the chilly grass. And bathed in the momentary glamour of the setting sun, the blond poet from Montréal, perhaps because of the way he walked, with muscular legs and forward-thrust pelvis, called up a vision for the old Greek poet. Suddenly what he saw before him was his elderly mistress glorified in gold and crossing an endless lawn on the arm of *le Roi Soleil.* In a flash of perception, he understood that the Laiah he knew, staggering through her life's eternal afternoon, must somehow have been translated long ago, before he ever knew her, from some other source and some completely different life.

Looking farther, the Greek noticed for the first time that beyond the suburbs and the industrial park, beyond the bridge

too, the skyline was nothing but treetops. A dark line of trees.
The forest, he supposed. Wild nature. This was a civilization
whose limits were quickly reached. And the daylight was going
too. Surely it was too cold for them to be kept out here for much
longer. Still hoping for the carpeted library and clutching at the
flaps of his coat, he turned around in his chair, straining to see
into the house. But the tall windows were filled with the black
reflections of tree branches, and instead he found himself looking directly at the English teacher behind him.

The oblique light revealed a man not young but younger
than the Greek, who felt that he should know this Englishman.
He was a rugged, inevitable figure of the academic landscape.
All over the world there were others like him, language carpet-
baggers following in the wake of conquest, industrial or economic. At least this one was struggling to understand. He and
the Serbian poet had resolved their language barrier by ignoring it.

'Who *is* that woman? Is she a poetess?' the Englishman was
asking.

There was an urgency in his voice, or testiness, or even
anger. It was the way he spat out the word *poetess*.

The Greek glanced into his eyes and observed that they were
a pale greenish grey with black pinpoints for pupils. A dangerous man perhaps. Well, of course, thought the Greek, who had
always known that northerners were basically barbarians, and
violent. Their schools were cruel and coercive. This man when
young would have been beaten. However he was no longer a
threat and certainly not to the Greek, who decided nevertheless
that this would be his last reading tour. He shifted around again,
hauling at his coat, and looked back to the others on the lawn.

Laiah had recovered her balance and now held the hand of
the blond poet. Out of her mask of courage, with a sort of tri-
umph, she was gazing around her. Then she smiled or seemed
to smile in the direction of her Greek lover.

While the young Serb, not much of a poet perhaps but making progress already, understood what the Englishman had said. He turned his millennial European gaze upon her and answered the question.

'Non,' he said, categorically, 'femme de poète ...'

To him it was obvious that she was a poet's wife.

The Greek smiled back at her and turned the collar of his coat up. His eyes fell to Laiah's small twisted hand, clasping the hand of the Sun King. In silhouette, their faces were hard for him to make out, yet he was sure that they were smiling. And as they walked across the lawn towards him, in the smoky haze of evening and autumn and the dusty pollen of chrysanthemums, through the coming darkness of this wild cold foreign country, their linked hands moved across a last flare of sunlight as it came lancing through between the trees. It, they, blazed in his vision and for an infinitesimal instant the Greek thought that he caught a glimpse of the first, the original Laiah. In that instant he believed that he understood at last.

He realized with a thrill of apprehension that there are those among us whose passage upon this earth is so full and perfect that it must be their final one. For them reincarnation would be pointless. When they are taken up into light they will pass into disembodied bliss and join the immortals – or that is what the old Greek poet thought, looking at Laiah. Then the same ray of light lit up the undrunk wine in his glass and dazzled him, so that he fumbled it and let it slip out of his fingers.

But dropping it, he was aware even before it had finished falling, before it spilled into the grass, of people turning, reaching out, of a collective gasp as others ran to help him. He was so glad. It was too cold now and too dark outside. The afternoon was over. At last they were going to take him inside, into the house where it was warm and where he could sit in an upholstered armchair with walls of books around him.

The Unknown Poet

The dream was so rich there was even a smell of earth and jungle flowers. Through patterns of yellow light and olive shade came the sounds of water dripping, and the piercing voices of strange birds. He was beginning to understand that it was a dream but was still burrowing into it, trying to gather its tendrils round him, when its fabric tore. Awake, not knowing why, he found himself in a dim room smelling of dust and his own clothing. Overhead was a greyish ceiling and seeping round the edges of the blind came the grey-white light of an unknown season. It was cold. With effort, he remembered. February, and still winter. This was Trois-Rivières and it was still winter. His ears ringing with bird calls and his sinuses dilated with flowery vapours, he rolled over and sat up on the edge of the mattress.

He reminded himself of his own name. Jean-Charles Murray. Thirty-seven years old. He lay down again closed his eyes. Was there a last gleam of silver water through the dark green? It vanished. Reality, what little there was of it, returned. He was out of work. And it was more or less daylight outside, therefore the night must be finished. He got up and off the mattress.

In the bathroom he weighed himself, shivering. Two hundred and seventeen pounds, heavy for five foot nine. He stepped off the scales and went to make coffee. There was no milk in the refrigerator, only a jar of mustard and a dry hot-dog bun. Jean-Charles wondered how he could continue to get heavier, living on coffee and beer and bread. His unemployment insurance was almost finished. There would be one more cheque, maybe two, he wasn't sure. Standing in front of the refrigerator's humming blue heart, he closed his eyes again and saw the flash of wings. He was still hearing passionate shrieks and smelling petal smells as he moved across to plug the kettle in. The jar of instant coffee was beside it, stuck to the counter, and he peered into the sludgy residue there.

When the kettle had boiled he rinsed out the coffee jar with the hot water and stood by the kitchen table to drink the thin brown liquid, listening to the building as it breathed, shifted and muttered around him. This was no jungle but a warren. There were five other flats in it and through the walls they sent him muffled messages of ordinary domesticity. He could hear people walking back and forth, snatches of television dramas, music, or the sounds of children arguing with their parents. Overhead and in the hall and the stairs to the street, different classes of footsteps came and went, mixed with bits of conversation, people reminding each other of where they were going and what they had to do while they were out.

'*Oublie-pas mon Tévé Hebdo.*'

Through the walls came sounds of doors and drawers opening and closing, water running, toilets being flushed, and sometimes something heavy being moved.

Whereas Jean-Charles made no noise at all. He slept, washed, drank coffee and went out, all in silence. Recently he hadn't gone out much. The cold had not let up for weeks. Through the window he saw cars dragging long tails of exhaust along the hard white surface of the road, the air too cold for the fumes to rise, while he stayed inside and tried to sleep the winter away. The landlord kept the heat at the legal minimum for the season and his bed was the warmest place to be.

Trois-Rivières was Jean-Charles's home town but his only reason for being here now was that it was cheaper than Montréal. His family, more or less English-speaking, had moved on. His father was dead, his brother was in Edmonton, and his mother was living with one of her sisters in Sudbury.

They had called him Chuck but now they were far away. He had a sister too but he wasn't sure where she was, probably somewhere in the States. There were still people he recognized here, sometimes he met and spoke with someone in the street, but in French. He had no close friends. For the few who did know him, he was always Jean-Charles.

He set his cup down, most of its contents still undrunk, as he took in the fact that the light *was* different today. It was grey, and not the fiery white of deep winter. There must be cloud out there and if there was cloud, that would mean that the cold had broken. The kitchen window opened into a rear shed whose panes had been closed over with plywood, so he padded into the front room and shifted the plastic curtain to look down into the rue des Volontaires. It was almost dark outside, the sky a dense and sombre colour that revealed no angle of light. What time was it? Anyway, it was certainly milder, it almost looked like rain. Then he saw the postman swing up the outside steps with a bundle of mail. So it would be about one o'clock. He heard the gust of air in the vestibule below, then the clunk of mail being slotted into the tenants' mail boxes. Six clunks for the six boxes. The man's back went down the steps and across the street. Maybe the second-last cheque had come. Jean-Charles needed it. He went to put on some clothes.

Back in the kitchen, he sat down at the table and sorted through a wad of advertising flyers in search of the envelope. It wasn't there. Instead there was a square one, looking something like an invitation, although of cheaper paper. He opened it and found a half sheet of paper folded once. This he turned over in his hands. At first it seemed, unreasonably, like another sort of advertisement. It was only slowly and with dull surprise that Jean-Charles began to understand what it was that he held in front of him. It was for him alone, not for anyone else, not for him and all his neighbours. Someone had sent this letter to him, personally. But what was it? He looked back at the envelope, then at the sheet of paper. No return address. No signature. Yet it had his name, Jean-Charles Murray, written right on it.

Beneath the written message there was a heart shape drawn in red ink. What on earth for? It was almost impossible for Jean-Charles to grasp the fact that this thing was a Valentine, or that it could be meant for him. He'd never had anything like it. Amazed, he put it down and looked again at the envelope. What was the date today? He counted back a few days to whenever it was that he had known the date. Yes, today must be about the fourteenth of February. It was a Valentine, and sent anonymously. Now he saw that his name on the envelope had also been written in red ink with a broad-nibbed pen. Why hadn't he noticed that before he opened it? But he excused himself for not noticing. The writing was too slick, too fluently personal, like the fake handwriting that the direct-mail advertisers use on their solicitations – *you have been selected by our team of specialists* – and that everyone tests with a wet finger. He hadn't tested it before but now he did. The ink ran.

At last he read the message, printed in capitals on a smallish rectangle of flimsy paper printed with faint blue lines in a grid. It had been torn off against a ruler in order to fit it into the envelope. And it said:

THO THOU THINKEST NOUGHT OF ME,
EVER FAITHFUL THINE I BE.
SHOULD I DON MY FINEST RAIMENT,
PERCHANCE I'D REAP, AS HIGHEST PAYMENT,
THY GLANCE, DIVESTED OF ITS SCORN,
TO KINDLE HOPE – YET UNBORN –
OF DAYS THAT I MIGHT CALL THEE MINE
AND DOTE UPON THEE, VALENTINE.

That part was written in black ink but underneath was the

heart, drawn with the broad-nibbed pen in red ink. 'Jean-Charles' was written across the heart and an elegant triple-fletched arrow punctured it with three little impact slashes. He turned the paper over again. It took him fifteen or twenty seconds more to realize that the message was written in English. How could this be? No one here spoke English to him any more. Most people didn't even remember that he came from a family who had spoken English. So who on earth?

Jean-Charles put the thing down, stood up and walked into the front room. He looked out the window again, then came back to the kitchen. Standing over the paper on the table, he observed that the heart was lopsided, the right ventricle facing him being bigger than the left. That would make it the left ventricle, and therefore anatomically correct. The arrow slanted downwards towards the left. Did that mean the person drawing it was left-handed? Or did it mean the opposite?

His next thought was that there was some kind of nastiness here, that someone was mocking him, trying to make a fool of him. Malevolence. He felt a pressure in his temples and a slow, slow thudding as his heart seemed to drop into an unexpected lower gear needed for hauling a heavy load. His blood pulsed in his fists as he gazed down at the paper, breathing slowly and deeply. He clutched the wooden back of the chair in front of him and leaned on it, feeling the flimsy crosspiece flex under his palms. His heart was returning to normal but he was still bending over the chair when he felt it give. For a split second it seemed to be slipping sideways when in fact it was coming apart in his hands. The bars of the back collapsed and dowelled bits of it skidded across the room. Jean-Charles fell against the table, his elbow knocking over the rest of his coffee and sending the various advertising flyers to the floor in a coloured flurry. At that the breathing of the house, the mutterings and shiftings and gushings fell silent for a moment.

Shuddering, he straightened up and exhaled a long breath

into the silence. He shoved the remains of the chair aside and picked the Valentine up out of the wreckage. The coffee had missed it. He held it closer to the ceiling light and looked again at the writing. Although it was in capital letters, the writer had obviously found them an effort and only the first two lines were really block-shaped. After that they sloped and flowed and began to reveal themselves. They looped, had long tails and gatherings and many downward slashes, but mostly to the right rather than to the left, unlike the arrow. He knew nothing about graphology but he observed these things and tried to understand them. Now he looked for other details. The writer had tried to keep the letters perpendicular but had not succeeded. And yet there was no consistent slant. One line lunged ahead and the next dragged its heels and leaned backwards. The strangest thing was that the message was in English.

It could still be someone French, he reasoned, who had copied this out of a book somewhere. It looked copied. No one French was likely to have written the poem, but how many English-speakers could have either? The verses could even have been miscopied. The sixth line seemed to him to be missing a syllable. It should have been TO KINDLE HOPE — AS YET UNBORN. A French speaker might have missed a word or not noticed the break in the scansion. And then, since nothing could be taken for granted, which sex was it, man or woman? The roundness of the letters looked feminine, but the disorder of the slant seemed masculine.

Suspicion returned as he stood amidst the wreckage. There must be something angry here. This had to be some sort of attack, aimed at unsettling him, but why? The only other possibility, unthinkable, undreamed of, was that there was a woman out there somewhere, a woman who was French — because of the paper lined in little squares — and who was in love with him. Jean-Charles stared at the red lettering on the envelope, large, looping, slightly backhanded. Must be a woman. This Valentine might be, it could be, real.

He laid the sheet of paper and the envelope on top of the refrigerator and rested his forehead against the door frame. When his head ached like this the barometric pressure was falling. He really should go out and buy food. There was a weather change coming. His back was starting to ache too, and his knees pained him. He kicked his way through the mess on the floor, pausing to turn off the light on his way out of the kitchen, and went back to bed, where he threw himself down in his clothes, wanting only to return to the jungle. The dream was long gone, however. Instead Jean-Charles fell into a heavy sleep.

And some time later – how long a time he did not know – he awoke suddenly, heaved off the bed in a single movement, and went once more to look out through the front window. Now he'd missed the day completely. It was dark again and yes, from the gleam on the sidewalks and the wires, he could see that a cold wetness was condensing out of the gloom. They called it an ice storm, this sullen glazing of everything, but there was nothing stormy about it. Instead the darkness over-head sank towards the earth while the temperature crept upwards to the freezing point. Then icy water dribbled meanly out of the blackness, sticking and hardening like some alien element, inexorably coating everything.

Jean-Charles was very hungry by this time and he turned away from the window. In the kitchen, he switched the light back on just long enough to avoid the pieces of broken chair and broken cup scattered on the floor while he retrieved the Valentine from the top of the fridge. He put it in his pocket. Then he put on his boots and his parka and went down the stairs and out. The sidewalk was coated with ice but there was relief, a sort of liberation, in feeling liquid rain again after all the weeks of arctic cold. Finding his footing by setting his feet flatly, not seeking traction, he tramped slowly down the rue des

Volontaires towards the centre of town. This street had been
named for the citizens who had rushed out to defend the town
against American invasion in 1776. They'd succeeded, too. The
revolutionaries had been driven out with anything to hand,
fowling pieces, kitchen knives, cast-iron pots and pans thrown
from windows. But that was over two hundred years ago. The
Americans were cleverer now. They bought the factories, then
closed them. There was no work. Again he wondered what time
it was. Sometimes the Pub-en-Ville gave out little hot sausages
for their happy hour.

Crossing the rue Royale, he looked out for traffic but saw
only a couple of cars crawling slowly away from him, down the
slope past the Café Morgane and the Bank of Nova Scotia.
Although freezing rain was congealing over everything, for
some reason the snowbanks between the concert hall and the
town hall had been shovelled aside. They'd opened a pathway
through to the Centre Culturel, where yesterday there had been
four feet of snow. Now the fresh snowbanks loomed ice-coated
on either side of a slicked path and he decided to cut through
there.

But instead Jean-Charles came face to face with a strange
little procession edging through the dark drizzle, a straggle of
sombre-coated figures clutching at each other's arms as they
advanced cautiously out of the Centre Culturel and along the
path of streaming ice. They were following in the wake of a tall
grey figure in a formal topcoat tailored to his stoop. The mayor.
They halted in a group and blocked the newly dug path, so that
Jean-Charles would have had to push through them to get
across to the rue des Forges and the Pub-en-Ville. What was
going on? It seemed to be some sort of ceremony, attended by
women of various ages and few men. Who would come out in
this weather – and for what?

The mayor, as sure-footed as Jean-Charles himself, had
paused and was waiting beside the concrete base of a tubular

metal structure that Jean-Charles had not seen before. How long had that thing been there? Blinding lights came on from different directions at once and he found that there were television cameras here too. The man in the tailored coat straightened and pivoted into their blaze like something heliotropic, smiling for the cameras with a practised squint while Jean-Charles stood at the back of the crowd to hear his speech.

The mayor informed his followers that the tubular structure of empty cubes was art. It was a sculpture and a memorial to poets. Inspired by the traditional monuments to the unknown soldier, it was intended, he said, to commemorate all those whose writings had been in vain.

It seemed to Jean-Charles that there must be something wrong with this idea and he tried to figure it out. Why was the unknown soldier unknown? Because he had committed crimes, killed his fellow men? No, it wasn't that. He was supposed to represent all those who had died, equally unknown, and been trodden into the muck of the battlefield, never identified or recognized for their common sacrifice. They were all equally tragic. But surely the unknown poet was in competition with other poets – and every one of them wanted to be known. That was their only battle, for individual recognition. The idea didn't make sense. A poet left his writings to identify him. Wasn't that why he wrote, wasn't the immortality of his name the whole point? Wasn't that one of the things that made him want to be a poet, in fact? Jean-Charles stood in the dark, shivering while he tried to sort it out.

Then there was movement at the far side of the crowd as something was handed forward. It occurred to Jean-Charles that poets who were unknown must find themselves in that position because they weren't very good. But now the mayor was talking about a bouquet of flowers, *'une gerbe de fleurs ... pour la Saint-Valentin.'* These people had come here to see him lay a bunch of flowers at the foot of this metal monstrosity because it was Valentine's Day. *Though thou thinkest nought of me, ever faithful, thine I be.* Anonymous poems for anonymous love. What good was anonymous love? And where were the poems anyway?

Jean-Charles realized he was staring into the barrette and blond chignon of a plump woman in a fur-lined *pelisse* who was standing just in front of him. Because he was so hungry, he could smell her extra clearly, her hair and perfume, warm damp Lusterized fur, and warm damp perfumed clothing and flesh under it. Icy rain water was dribbling into his collar and when he stepped back from her he put a foot into the edge of the snowbank. Slush ran into his boot. At the same time there was a contrary movement among the poetry enthusiasts. They were pushing forward to witness the act of deposition, and he got past behind them and escaped around the corner and down the steps into the rue des Forges. *Should I don my finest raiment ...* he thought, huddling into his parka, wiping black rain from his eyes as he walked and slid, more carefully than before, towards the pub. Yet Jean-Charles felt faintly happy for the first time that day. After all, someone *had* sent him a Valentine. He didn't have to stand around at silly cultural events for human contact. For whatever reason, he'd had a sign. What he really needed was a beer, however, and something to eat. When he reached the corner of the rue Notre-Dame, he found that the Pub-en-Ville was closed for renovations. He leaned close to see in through the wet dark glass of the door. There was no hot food after all, there was nothing in there but dust and darkness and ladders. Shivering more, he pulled the hood of his parka up around his ears and turned to stare across Notre-Dame and down the rue des Forges towards the blackness that was the winter sky over the waters of the St Lawrence River. At the foot of the street, by the port, he saw lights on at the Club Saint-Paul. Maybe he could afford a beer or two there.

Going down des Forges the sidewalk was so slippery that he

left it and walked in the middle of the street where there were faint traces of grit spread for the wheels of cars. Most of that was iced over by now and, starting down the slope, he almost lost his footing. He slithered and corrected while at the same instant his ears caught the smallest swishing sound behind him. And before he could quite turn, there was something greyish right there, right on him.

A small car. Jean-Charles jumped, but slipped. No one could have said whether he hit the car or it hit him. Probably it was he who slid into the side of it, a rusty Renault, but the car itself was already out of control. He clutched at a door-handle and some part of the windshield, and his weight turned the little machine completely around. He and it slid down the slope in a revolving tangle, Jean-Charles following it on one knee, hampered by his heavy boots and his parka, until it came to rest on the quayside railroad tracks, a few yards from the water. From inside the car came screams, short and sharp, reviving memories of the jungle dream. When the car stopped, so did the screams. They were still several car lengths from the edge and the lethal waters of the St Lawrence but for the empty second or two after they came to a halt, Jean-Charles could hear, with crystalline clarity, the chinking, crunching, businesslike jostle of the ice floes pushing past in the river.

The woman inside the car must be in shock. She was sitting frozen, clutching the wheel, staring whitely at him through the side window. He stared back, ceasing to hear the river sounds and seeing instead that she was the blonde who had stood in front of him back there at the ceremony for the unknown poet. *Perchance I'd reap, as highest payment, thy glance, divested of its scorn.* Painfully, he tested his knee and stood up. Nothing was broken. His hand was still on the handle, so he opened the car door. What should he say to her? She shrank back a little. *'Vous n'êtes pas blessée?'* he asked her, finally. Was she hurt?

There was still a silence. Her mouth moved but no words

came out. Then she found her voice. *'Non, non … mais Monsieur, vous-même, vous …'* After all, it was her car that had hit him, more or less. Then she was trying to explain to him that the brakes had failed. Jean-Charles almost laughed at that. The brakes?

'Your car was sliding, Madame, the road's covered with ice. No, I am not hurt, or at least I don't think so.'

She began to tremble and sniff. She said that her wrist hurt, her back hurt, her neck hurt and *'Oh, mon doux Seigneur,'* she was too shaken up to drive after this.

'Shall I call the police,' he asked her, 'should we report it as an accident?'

That alarmed her. *'Non, non,'* since he wasn't hurt, but …

'But what, Madame?'

'Perhaps, perhaps if it was not an imposition …'

'Perhaps what?'

Well, she was afraid of trying to back the car out of its present position. What if it went straight into the river? She didn't know what to do.

'Okay,' he said, 'okay.'

Flopping and tugging at her *pelisse*, she was already climbing over the gear shift to leave him the driver's seat. *'Par-là,'* she said, *'j'habite juste ici …'*

She lived just around the corner, in one of the new apartment blocks put up between Notre-Dame and the paper company's warehouses on the river. With Jean-Charles's weight in it, her car had a better grip on the road. He backed it off the tracks, avoided the deep wet snowbank left by the snow-plough and drove it to her building. It turned out that she was afraid of the wet slope to her underground garage as well, so he drove it in there for her.

'If I leave it outside it won't start,' she said.

In the garage, they both climbed out of the Renault and looked at each other over its roof. *'Peut-être, je sais pas moi,'* she said. '... *peut-être ... vous aimeriez prendre un bon café chaud...?*' After the cold and the wet and the shock, a hot coffee.

Jean-Charles's stomach rumbled as he accepted.

In a hot, dry apartment filled with black-and-white lacquered things, she turned on a lot of lights, then took his parka and hung it on a lacquered hook. She shook and adjusted her fur-lined coat and buttoned it onto a coat hanger, stroking it down. Then she stepped into the little kitchen and took a package of coffee beans out of the freezer.

'You're not from around here,' she said over the snarl of the coffee-grinder.

Jean-Charles, from the opening between kitchen and the dining area, turned to stare at his own bulky image in the black reflections from her big windows. How did they do it? Everyone said that he had no accent in French but she had detected something, what? She brought the coffee in and set down cups on a little table by the window, overlooking the dim outlines of the paper shed roofs. Beyond were the ice floes, not visible in the dark, and beyond that, faintly over the black water, the lights of Sainte-Angèle-de-Laval on the south shore.

'Well, actually', he said, 'I was born in Trois-Rivières, but my parents were English.'

'Isn't that funny,' she said. 'My name is Clara. It sounds English but I'm not. What's your name?'

'Jean-Charles,' he said, wondering why they were using first names only.

'So you have a French name. And you're from here and I'm not. I'm from Québec City.'

Jean-Charles was putting cream and sugar into his cup. He picked it up and steadied it in its saucer with his other hand. When he tasted the coffee he found it very rich and strong. The heat of it and the heat of the room made him almost dizzy. This place was even warmer than a bar would have been. And Clara looked at his thick hand, still blue with cold and displaying a dark red bruise along the outer side and up the wrist. His nails were clean but her porcelain cup trembled in the blunt fingers.

'I've been working here for a year now,' she said. 'For the Ministère des Affaires culturelles. I was transferred here, I didn't know anybody.'

'You were at that thing,' he said. 'I saw you at that ceremony behind the library.'

She looked away from him. 'Ah, yes, with the local writers' group and the mayor. Yes. It's Valentine's Day, did you know that?'

'Yes, I did,' he said. 'I did know that. Because I got a Valentine today. But I don't know who sent it.'

'That's the way it's supposed to be,' she told him. 'A Valentine is supposed to be anonymous.'

She looked more curiously at him and drank a sip of coffee. He stared down at her grey nylon carpet.

'You're lucky,' she said. 'All I got was a card from the agent that rented me this apartment ... and one from the director of personnel telling me how much he appreciated my work.'

Jean-Charles said nothing.

'What do you do,' she asked him.'

'Nothing,' he said, swallowing the last of his coffee. 'I had a job in the Maritimes and when that finished I came back here.'

He didn't tell her that he'd worked counselling unemployed fishermen, telling them how to become hairdressers and computer programmers. He wished he knew how to become a hairdresser or a programmer himself.

'You'll find something,' she said. 'Because you're lucky. You can speak English.'

'Not much help in Trois-Rivières,' he said. 'Not much luck either.' The porcelain cup rattled in its saucer as he reached out to set it down, hoping that its noise had covered the sound of his stomach rumbling.

At that Clara set her own cup down and stood up. *'Écoutez,'* she said, 'why don't you stay and have supper with me? There isn't much in the fridge, but I'll throw something together, you know, *à la bonne franquette*, you'd be very welcome ... after nearly running you down with my car ... it's the least I can offer you.'

Back she went to her kitchenette and her freezer. Out of it and into the microwave oven went frozen steaks and frozen French fries. She was making salad and talking through the archway about what a dead place Trois-Rivières was. Jean-Charles sat hunched over the coffee table and stared some more at his reflection in the glass of the windows. While he was wondering if she might have beer in her fridge, she suddenly reappeared beside him and handed him a glass of Scotch with ice cubes in it. *'Un petit whisky,'* she said, *'comme apéro, pourquoi pas?'* He accepted it and drank it, hearing kitchen machines whirring and clicking, then a cork popping. *'Voilà!'* she said, arriving back, this time to the black lacquer dining table at the end of the room. She put down two small bowls of pale green creamy soup, steaming, sprinkled with something. Somehow there were already napkins and glasses and plates and cutlery. She lit candles and gave him a silver soup spoon.

'This is amazing,' he said. 'Thank you.'

'It's nothing, it's nothing,' she insisted, 'just whatever I could throw together.'

She poured a small quantity of dark red wine into his glass and invited him to taste it. He did. He found it musky and flatly astringent, not really pleasant.

'It may be too cold,' she said. 'I hope it's not too cold.'

'I don't know,' he said.

She became anxious. 'It's supposed to be a good bottle,' she said, pouring herself some, sniffing it.

Understanding that he was supposed to approve, Jean-Charles swirled the stuff around in his glass. It coated the inner surface. He told her he was sure it'd be all right when it had warmed up a bit and she smiled. She came and filled his glass properly, then she sat down across the corner of the table from him. *'À la Saint-Valentin!'* she said, a little too brightly, lifting her own glass.

As Jean-Charles spooned his way through the creamed lettuce soup, wondering what he was eating, she told him. She even gave him the recipe.

'I'm sorry it's so simple,' she said, 'really I never entertain. Nobody ever comes here. I'm totally alone in this town.'

'So am I,' said Jean-Charles.

While he was eating steak and potatoes, she explained that she hadn't planned to come to Trois-Rivières, because she'd been hoping to be posted to to Québec's Délégation générale in Paris, but that her contact there had let her down. *'C'était mon ancien chum,'* she confessed, pouring herself more wine. He was her former boyfriend. She had thought that they were still good friends but somehow they weren't.

'Maybe you should have sent him a Valentine,' said Jean-Charles.

'Maybe he should have sent me one,' she replied, filling Jean-Charles's glass again.

'What I want to know,' said Jean-Charles, 'is who sent me that Valentine. Who's got my address? That's what I want to know.'

'You may never find out,' she said. 'But men are so lucky. *C'est facile pour vous-autres, les hommes ...* It's easy for a man, you can always find another girlfriend, there are so many lonely women. It's not like that for us, you know. My phone never rings, nobody invites me anywhere.'

The pupils of her eyes darkened and her lips began to tremble.

'You know, I tried,' she said. 'I did try, when I first came to this rotten little town. I invited colleagues, I gave dinners, but no one ever invited me back. What's wrong with me?'

She stared at him accusingly.

'I don't know,' said Jean-Charles.

'There's just absolutely nothing for an unmarried woman to do here in the evenings. I just work and come home and watch television and get up in the morning and go back to work.'

'I wish I could do that,' he said. 'I wish I had a job to go to. I wish I had a television set.'

Clara ignored that remark. Instead she stood up and went to the kitchen, slightly unsteady, and brought back a garlicky-smelling salad and a second bottle of wine, together with the corkscrew, which she handed to him. As he opened it, she gathered up the steak plates and took them away, and he looked at her legs. She was plump but her legs tapered down to small, fine ankles and pointed little feet.

She sat down again and leaned on the corner of the table, serving him salad with jerky gestures, splashing his wrist with vinaigrette. Then she held out her glass for more wine.

'You're not supposed to drink wine with salad like this,' she informed him, 'but who cares? It's such good wine. My old boyfriend got it for me from France at a special price. So he's paying for this. Here in Québec this wine costs thirty dollars a bottle but we might as well drink it, celebrate, why not? We've already had our car accident today, haven't we?'

Jean-Charles poured himself some more too. He wasn't sure how much of it he'd actually swallowed, but it did seem to improve as he kept drinking. Indifferent to gastronomic concerns, he finished the salad in three mouthfuls.

'You were hungry,' she said, planting both elbows on the table, watching him eat.

'Yes,' he said.

'I wish there was something for dessert,' she said, 'but I never keep anything like that in the house. I think there might be some marc de Bourgogne.'

She leaned farther across the corner of the table at him.

Jean-Charles was drunk with the food and the heat as well as the alcohol, but he could see that she was drunker. She smelled of the kitchen now, and of her musky wine. Her head wobbled and one of her eyes was drifting aside, diverging from its partner. Fascinated, he was staring into that divergence when her elbow slipped off the table. She'd lost her balance was falling off her chair when he caught her and at the same moment, in a different decision, simply thrust her to the floor and went down on top of her.

He'd forgotten how flimsy their bodies were. She was almost as tall as he was, and fat, so that she looked big and solid, but as she struggled with him, she seemed to weigh no more than some feather bolster. She was just fluff and marshmallow. The wine and the warmth, the red meat and the smell of her filled his mind with an auburn mist and his ears with a brassy ringing. Through that he heard tropical birds again, then the shrieks that had come from inside her Renault, and finally he realized that she was screaming underneath him and trying to push him off.

Oh, right. Remotely, he felt her scratching at his face. This was supposed to be wrong. It was illegal. He heaved aside, looked at her, and got up.

'Excuse me, forgive me,' he said. 'I forgot what I was doing.'

'Get out,' she screamed, *'Va t'en, va t'en, va t'en!* Get out of here and never come back.'

She was sitting on the floor hugging herself with her arms as she screamed, her eyes round and staring whitely, both of them back in focus.

And he backed away with his head pounding and his heart dropping into that lower gear again. Then he had his coat on, and his boots. Had he ever had a tuque or gloves? Maybe not. Anyway, he was through the door already and walking down a corridor, with the screams following him.

Now it was late, he didn't know how late, but after midnight and he was out on the street again. The scratches on his face stung him and he was seized with a feeling of dread. Would she call the police? When the car pulled alongside, the scratches would mark him as the would-be rapist.

Well, he thought, I'll confess to it all, anything. Let them lock me up. Why not? What have I got to do tomorrow or the next day or forever?

But no police car appeared. The town was utterly, totally silent. The sleet had stopped but nothing was moving because the whole world was coated with a half-inch of ice. It was almost impossible to move without slipping. Slowly, he shuffled and slithered north towards Notre-Dame. He found that his knee did hurt where he'd run into her car, and was starting to stiffen and throb with real pain. Since there was no traffic, he limped into the middle of the street and walked in the traffic lane once more. There was absolutely no one else out and it was the only way. It was bitterly cold now too. The ice was like iron.

As he made his way along the path past the Centre Culturel, he looked again at the monument to the unknown poet. Where was the bunch of flowers that the mayor had been about to lay at its base? Even that was gone. Someone must have swiped them already, and a good thing too, rather than let them freeze out here. But when Jean-Charles lifted his eyes to the metal superstructure, he saw where they were. It wasn't a bunch of flowers anyway, it was a potted plant, a wretched fern and something else stuck together into a plastic pot with a hook. The city employee who had shovelled the walk must have come out here with a ladder after everyone had gone home. He'd climbed up and hooked the thing high onto one of the pipes of the sculpture, out of the way of pilferers, and there it hung inside the empty cube, silhouetted coldly against the dark sky, coated with ice, sealed to the metal, dead. Jean-Charles was reminded of La Corriveau hung up to die of exposure in an iron cage at the crossroads. That was for poisoning her husband, as he recalled.

And there were no poems, except for the Valentine, which he discovered under his fingers in the bottom of his pocket. He pulled it out and held it up towards the streetlight to read the end of it.

> *To kindle hope – as yet unborn –*
> *Of days that I might call thee mine*
> *And dote upon thee, Valentine.*

Then he crumpled it into a ball and dropped it at the foot of the metal monument. There was no unknown poet buried under the steel structure, nor even any poems, and only the murdered plant hanging there.

As for whoever had sent the Valentine, well, all that meant was that at least one person somewhere in this strange, secretive little city remembered him, remembered his family possibly, and knew that he spoke English. Moreover it was someone whom he, Jean-Charles, had completely forgotten, thus proving that the person must be even lonelier than he was. He was never going to know who had sent the poem anyway. A Valentine was supposed to be anonymous, she'd told him that much. And unknown poets were unknown because they'd all been trodden into the muck of words. Maybe it was a war, after all. At the least the mayor, with literary-political astuteness, had chosen the one logical day on which to honour him.

His ears flaming with the pain of the cold and his aching hand shoved deep into his pocket, Jean-Charles crossed Notre-Dame and limped on up the rue des Volontaires. Dessert, she'd said. What was marc de Bourgogne anyway? He was nearly home. Maybe the police would come for him tomorrow. She could certainly find out who he was. He was known, he was identifiable, the Valentine had taught him that as well. But would she bother, tomorrow? Was what he had done so very bad? At the street door of his *logement* he stopped to feel in his other pocket for his key and stood listening for a moment. But there was no sound of any car coming, nothing, and the house itself, like the town, was quiet, all its mutterings and shiftings silenced for the night.

Jean-Charles straightened his back and took a deep breath. Then he did hear something. He was not completely alone after all because he could hear, from over the housetops, a scraping, hacking, chipping sound. He knew what it was. Understanding its cause gave the little noise a special intimacy. There was at least one other person still out in the cold, because back there in the laneway behind the houses, a late-night driver was trying to break through the icy carapace that had sealed his car shut. Chip, chip. *To kindle hope, as yet unborn.* Someone else just trying to get home. Clearly, through the ice-cold blackness came the small persistent sound of hopeful human purpose.

Born in Nova Scotia, Judith Cowan grew up in Toronto and was educated at the University of Toronto and l'Université de Strasbourg, France. She has lived in Trois-Rivières for many years and has translated the work of a wide range of Québec poets, including Gérald Godin, Yves Préfontaine and Yves Boisvert. Her previous story collection, *More Than Life Itself,* was shortlisted for the Québec Writers' Federation First Book Award.